Maryland General Assembly

Investigation by the Joint Committee on Public Buildings

into Certain Charges Preferred by Dr. J.S. Conrad, Late Superintendent and

Treasurer of the Maryland Hospital for the Insane at Spring Grove

Maryland General Assembly

Investigation by the Joint Committee on Public Buildings
into Certain Charges Preferred by Dr. J.S. Conrad, Late Superintendent and Treasurer of the Maryland Hospital for the Insane at Spring Grove

ISBN/EAN: 9783337382667

Printed in Europe, USA, Canada, Australia, Japan

Cover: Foto ©Andreas Hilbeck / pixelio.de

More available books at **www.hansebooks.com**

[Document Q.]

BY THE SENATE,

March 28th, 1878.

Read, and two hundred copies ordered to be printed.

By order,

AUGUSTUS GASSAWAY,

Secretary.

INVESTIGATION

BY THE

Joint Committee on Public Buildings

INTO CERTAIN CHARGES PREFERRED BY

DR. J. S. CONRAD,

LATE SUPERINTENDENT AND TREASURER OF THE

MARYLAND HOSPITAL FOR THE INSANE

AT SPRING GROVE.

ANNAPOLIS:

GEO. COLTON, PRINTER TO THE GENERAL ASSEMBLY.

1878.

INDEX.

.·—·.

REPORT.

To the Honorable, the Senate and House of Delegates:

The report of undersigned members of the Joint Standing Committee of the Senate and House of Delegates upon Public Buildings, in the matter of certain charges made by Dr. Conrad, late Superintendent of the Maryland Hospital for the Insane, situated at Spring Grove, against Dr. C. W. Chancellor, President of the Board of Managers of said Institution, respectfully beg leave to report to your honorable bodies that, after having diligently examined all the witnesses, and carefully considered all the evidence adduced before them, they find that, since the organization of the present Board of Managers under the act of 1876, and the selection by them of Dr. Conrad as Superintendent, the said institution has been better conducted, and many improvements have been made under its present management, and your committee say that it is much to be regretted that within the last four months disagreements have arisen, amongst the officers of said institution which have caused the resignation of Dr. Conrad; and your committee are of the opinion that the present charges were the outgrowth of said disagreements, and that this investigation was instigated by the feeling they engendered.

The facts charged upon the one side, and either admitted on the other or established by the evidence, contain nothing in themselves reprehensible, and your committee are unable to discover any improper motive actuating the officer charged in his official conduct.

All of which is respectfully submitted.

JOHN H. COOPER,
HERMAN STUMP, Jr.,
WILLIAM M. KNIGHT,
FRANK BROWN.

It will be seen that of the ten members from the above committee, only four sign the accompanying report.

CHARGES.

1. That he has endeavored to convert his position of honor and trust, as a member of the board, to one of personal emolument, by "canvassing the individual members of the board for his own appointment as the chief medical officer of the hospital (salary implied), stating that an officer resident at the hospital could not control the institution, in consequence of intimate association with subordinates." Witness, Dr. Thos. R. Brown.

2. That, failing in this, he has adroitly and persistently converted the patronage of the hospital to his own political advantage, and in doing so has violated the by-laws. In the absence of the chairman (Mr. Gunther) of the purchasing committee, he directed the superintendent to transfer the purchases of groceries from Stump & Son, wholesale dealers, of whom he had been ordered to obtain them by Mr. Gunther, to Schawgo, a small retail dealer residing in his own ward and next door to Dr. Chancellor's own dwelling, and when the superintendent failed by intention to make the transfer, he (Dr. Chancellor) ordered the steward, Mr. Brown, to make the change, which was done. These purchases amount to from two hundred and fifty to three hundred and fifty dollars a month. Witnesses, Dr. Conrad, Mr. Brown and Mr. Gunther.

3. That he ordered the purchase of carpets to be transferred from Turnbull Brothers, where the superintendent was ordered to obtain them by Mr. Gunther, to G. S. Griffith & Sons, and subsequently countermanded the order, stating to me as a reason, that "Mr. Griffith had refused to give him a letter of indorsement of his late report on almshouses." Witness, Dr. Conrad.

4. That he directed the change of tobacco purchases to be transferred from Werdebaugh & Co. to Mr. Dillehunt,

for political services to him, and subsequently countermanded the order for personal reasons. Witness, Dr.
Conrad.

5. That he ordered the stationery and printing to be transferred from Kelly & Piet to Dulancy, stating as a reason
that the latter had given him one hundred dollars to aid in
his election, (Sept., '77.) Witness, Dr. Conrad.

6. That he purchased two horses from parties living in
his own ward without authority of the committee or board.
Witness, Dr. Brown.

7. That he ordered repairs and improvements to be made
by parties of his own selection, without reference to the
executive committee. Witnesses, John W. McCoy, Dr.
Conrad and others.

8. That he has contemplated and expressed his determination to have the number of the present Board of Managers changed by legislative enactment, so as to get rid of
such members of the board as opposed him. Witness, Dr.
Conrad.

9. That he has not visited the hospital in the last four
months past.

10. That he ordered the superintendent to employ a colored man living in his ward, as a waiter at the board dinners, instead of the one before employed. Witnesses, Dr.
Conrad and Mr. Brown.

11. That he also ordered the superintendent to purchase
oysters of this same man, instead of Mr. Contee, where
they had formerly been obtained. Witness, Dr. Conrad.

12. That he has, on several occasions, ordered shipments
of flowers and plants from the hospital green-house to be
boxed up and expressed to his country residence in Virginia.

13. That he has ordered the superintendent to retain and
admit into the hospital a lunatic patient without warrant of
the law and ordinances, in deference to the wishes of one
of his constituents.

INVESTIGATION.

MARCH 18, 1878.

The Joint Committee on Public Buildings met at 4.30 P. M., in the room of the President of the Senate. Present, Senators Bannon and Stump, and Delegates Acton, Knight, Sander and Houston.

Dr. John S. Conrad was present to make a statement in regard to the causes which led to his resignation of the office of Medical Superintendent and Treasurer of the Maryland Hospital for the Insane. The witness was not sworn, the committee not being empowered to administer oath.

THE WITNESS SAID:

I have been connected with the hospital four years next August. I was resident physician to July, 1876; since then, medical superintendent and treasurer. It is my duty, under the act of 1876, to make a report to be transmitted to the Governor in December of each year. The fiscal year ends November 1. I should state that the Board of Managers used to require my monthly and quarterly reports to be made the second Tuesday after the expiration of each month or quarter. I found it difficult to do this, and asked for three weeks, which the board granted. At the end of the fiscal year the report for the whole year must be made out. I was granted one week to do this by the President, Dr. Chancellor. I said that it was utterly impossible to have the report ready within so short a time. He then gave me two weeks. I still said that it was impossible to get up the accounts of the departments and prepare the report in that time. I said that I was allowed three weeks to get up the monthly and quarterly reports, and why should I not have at least that much time now. He said the Governor wanted the reports sent in early. I pointed out that the law said that the report was to be made during the month of December. He, however, still insisted that I should have it ready within that time. At the meeting of the board two weeks after, the report of the President was ready. It was read to me, and I received the impression that I was not to cover its topics in my report. I thought that it covered the Superintendent's report. I considered it, therefore, as professionally discourteous, but said nothing. I did say, however, that it would not bear criticism. I said to Dr. Chancellor: "You say that ninety per cent. of insane persons can be cured in hospitals. That is not true, for statistics show that only about thirty per cent. are curable." He said: "I don't care: I won't change it; it would be too much trouble to alter my calculations." At that time not a single department had its report made up, nor was my report ready, and, heretofore, the President's report has been made up after these reports have been made.

MR. KNIGHT:

Could not Dr. Chancellor have made up his report from the monthly and quarterly reports?

DR. CONRAD:

Those reports are never used for the preparation of the annual report, and were all locked up in my safe at the time.

WITNESS, CONTINUING:

The Board of Managers adopted the president's report. When my report was submitted, it was at once seen that they did not agree at all, and there was a collision, and portions of mine were expunged.

MR. BANNON:

Have you those suppressed portions, Doctor?

The witness read from and filed with the committee the document marked "1 A."

MR. KNIGHT:

Was there a full board present when those portions were expunged?

THE WITNESS:

There was, sir. My report was read, and it was at once

seen that it was at variance with the president's report. A committee consisting of Messrs. Compton, McCoy, and Governor Bradford, were appointed to wait upon me in regard to the matter. Mr. Compton said that it was impossible to forward both reports to the Legislature. I said that the error of the board was in adopting the president's report before having seen the reports of the departments. This remark gave great offence to Dr. Chancellor. The committee asked me to withdraw my report and modify it. This I declined to do, stating that it was my duty under the by-laws to make just such a report as I had done, and asked that the whole report might be spread upon the minutes. I said I would not withdraw the report, stating that I had done my duty, and it was at their disposal. At first no objection was made to my request that the report should go upon the minutes, but I was afterwards requested to make amends for what I had said. The committee brought the matter to my attention, and the improprieties of which I was accused was, first, that I had said that it was improper for the board to adopt the report of the president in advance of the report of the superintendent; and, secondly, that I had demanded that the suppressed portions should go upon the minutes. A letter was drawn up, which I agreed to sign, regretting that the remarks had been made since they caused offence. That letter went on the minutes of the board; the committee reported to the board, and I understood that it was perfectly satisfactory to the board, when, I was informed, Dr. Chancellor stepped up and said: "I am not satisfied; I will be satisfied with nothing else than his resignation." But there were underlying causes for this determination to oust me, which I will state if the committee desire to hear.

A discussion arose in the committee as to whether the examination should proceed in the absence of the persons concerned by the testimony of the witness. The witness said:

I would prefer that Dr. Chancellor and Mr. Compton should be here. I prefer to reserve what I still have to give until I can give it in their presence.

The committee decided that the witness should proceed.

MR. KNIGHT:

Why was not this matter stated at the time of the visit of the committee to the hospital?   •

WITNESS:

The report was not then published.

MR. KNIGHT:

Why did they object to your report?

WITNESS:

For the reasons I have stated. Mr. Compton stated to me: If this report is sent in you will get no appropriation. I give this as the principle underlying the suppression of portions of my report. The other portion of what I wish to say to the committee concerns the causes of my resignation. After the difficulties referred to had occurred, Dr. Chancellor did not come to the hospital for four months; that is to say, from the second week in November, when my report was suppressed, until after my resignation, December 9. Now, I wish to show what Dr. Chancellor's principal object was in not being satisfied with my letter of apology when the rest were. His reason was that he wanted the position of Medical Superintendent for himself. Dr. Thomas Brown, of the board, has told me that Dr. Chancellor canvassed the board for his own appointment to the place, after its organization under the act of 1876, but as the law forbade compensation to any member of the board, and hence his election was impossible, I was elected. Dr. Chancellor told me last summer, that he designed to have a bill passed by Mr. Gorman, which would remove the present organization and make such changes as would be material. He said he wanted to get rid of certain members of the board who opposed him in certain measures. The bill is the one on the Senate file—No. 45, I think. I told Dr. Thom and Dr. Brown last November, of this, and that it was Dr. Chancellor's object to oust me from the management. Dr. Thom told Dr. Chancellor of this, but he did not make any charges against me then. Now, why didn't he? There was something, which if not true, would have justified them in dismissing me. The appearance of the bill now justifies my statement made then. Dr. Chancellor had previously told me that he intended to get a bill passed to create the office of Inspector of Public Charities, and that it would be provided that when the services of that officer should not be required for that special duty, his services should be given entirely to the hospital. He asked me for the Canadian act establishing the office held by Mr. Langmuir. I spoke to Dr. Broome, my assistant, about the matter, and remarked that some of Dr. Chancellor's friends ought to advise him against it.

The witness then read portions of and submitted the whole of the following memorandum of charges against Dr. Chancellor:

1st. That he has endeavored to convert his position of honor and trust, as a member of the board, to one of personal emolument, by canvassing the individual members of the board for his own appointment as the chief medical officer of the hospital, (salary implied), stating that an officer resident at the hospital could not control the institution in consequence of intimate associations with the subordinates. Witness, Dr. Thomas R. Brown.

2nd. That failing in this, he has adroitly and persistently converted the patronage of the hospital to his own political advantage, and, in doing so, has violated the by-laws. (See page 7, section Purchasing Committee). To specify: He directed the superintendent, in the absence of the chairman of the Purchasing Committee (Mr. Gunther), to transfer the purchases of groceries from Stump & Son (wholesale dealers), of whom the superintendent had been ordered to obtain them by Mr. Gunther, to Schawgo, a small retail dealer, residing in his own ward, and next door to Dr. Chancellor's own dwelling, and when the superintendent intentionally failed to make the transfer, he (Dr. Chancellor) ordered the steward, Mr. Brown, to make the change, which was done. These purchases amount to from two hundred and fifty dollars to three hundred and fifty dollars per month. Witnesses, Dr. Conrad, Mr. Brown and Mr. Gunther.

3d. That he ordered the purchases of carpets to be transferred from Turnbull Bros., where the superintendent was ordered to obtain them (by Mr. Gunther), to G. S. Griffith & Sons. and subsequently countermanded the order. stating to me, as a reason, that Mr. Griffith had refused to give him a letter of endorsement of his late report on almshouses. Witness, Dr. Conrad.

4th. That he directed the change of tobacco purchases to be transferred from Werdebaugh & Co. to Mr. Dillehunt. for political services to him, and subsequently countermanded the order for personal reasons. Witness. Dr. Conrad.

5th. That he ordered the stationery and printing to be transferred from Kelly & Piet to Dulaney, stating as a reason that the latter had given him one hundred dollars to aid in his election. (September, 1877.) Witness, Dr. Conrad.

6th. That he purchased two horses from parties living in his ward, without authority of the committee or board. Witness, Dr. Brown.

7th. That he ordered repairs and improvements to be made by parties of his own selection. without reference to the Executive Committee. (See page 7, by-laws, section "Executive Committee.") Witnesses, Mr. John W. McCoy, Dr. Conrad and others.

8th. That he has contemplated and expressed his determination to have the number of the present Board of Managers changed by legislative enactment so as to get rid of such members of the board as opposed him. Witness, Dr. Conrad.

9th. That he has not visited the hospital in the last four (4) months past. Witnesses, all the officers.

10th. That he ordered the superintendent to employ a colored man living in his ward as a waiter at the board dinners, instead of the one before employed. Witnesses, Dr. Conrad and Mr. Brown.

11th. That he ordered the superintendent to purchase oysters of this same man instead of Mr. Contee, where they had formerly been obtained. Witness, Dr. Conrad.

12th. That he has. on several occasions, ordered ship-

ments of flowers and plants from the hospital green-house
to be boxed and expressed to his country residence in Virginia.

13th. That he has ordered the superintendent to retain
and admit into the hospital a lunatic patient, without warrant of the law and ordinances, in deference to the wishes
of one of his constituents.

MR. KNIGHT:

Were there not certain charges brought against Dr. Broome
by you that led to your resignation?

WITNESS.

My assistant, Dr. Broome, was quite insubordinate, and I
noted a number of instances. Dr. Chancellor refused to
hold any communication with me, which also made him insubordinate to me. I finally submitted charges to the board.
I asked that the witnesses should be sworn, but this was refused. While the witnesses were being examined by the
board, the proceedings could be plainly overheard. I could
not help hearing, as, owing to Mr. Farnandis' deafness, witnesses had to speak loud. I thought the mode of conducting
the examination an outrage. I had been told by a member
of the board that my resignation would be demanded. I
did not intend to anticipate that demand; in fact, I had said
I would not; but I then made up my mind to hand it in.
That was the direct but not the remote cause. The board
decided all the charges to be unsustained, except the eighth
and ninth, although every item of the seventeenth was
admitted by Dr. Broome.

Upon motion of Mr. Stump, the clerk of the committee
was directed to notify the Board of Managers and Mr. G.
S. Griffith to attend the next meeting of the committee.
Dr. Conrad was also notified to be in attendance. The committee then adjourned until Wednesday afternoon at four
o'clock.

MARCH 20, 1878.

The committee met pursuant to adjournment, Senator Bannon in the chair. Present, a quorum of the committee.

Dr. J. S. Conrad, sworn and examined.

By Mr. COMPTON:

Q. Please state about what time those flowers were sent that are mentioned in the twelfth charge?

A. I can't tell the exact date.

Q. Can you not approximate it?

A. The first lot was sent during Mr. Hall's time, about the time of the Doctor's nomination. Mr. Hall is now dead. The second lot has been by the present gardener, Mr. Watson. I think that was about this time last year, as well as I remember.

By Dr. CHANCELLOR:

Q. Was the board organized at that time?

A. No, sir.

Q. Did I have authority to send anything from the hospital at that time?

A. No, I do not know that you did. You told Mr. Hall that you would like to have some plants, and I suppose, in order to gratify you, Mr. Hall sent them.

Q. Had I ever seen Mr. Hall before, that you know of?

A. Not that I know of.

Q. Do you know what those plants were worth?

A. I cannot tell you; I do not know the value of plants. I know that Mr. Hall had been in the habit of selling the plants to the neighbors, and from the sale of the plants the green-house had been more than supported, which has never been the case since his death.

Q. Did you sanction the selling of them?

A. I assisted Mr. Hall in putting them up and shipping them. I would state in that connection that other members of the board have ordered things before, but in every instance I have sent them a bill, which has been paid in every instance.

Q. What other members of the board?

A. Governor Bradford ordered two pigs at one time, which were sent to him. I never said anything to him about the pay and never sent him the bill, but he came and paid it himself. I think the same is the case with Mr. Gunther. I never sent a bill to him and never directed Mr. Brown to do so.

By Mr. COMPTON:

Q. Did not Dr. Chancellor offer to pay for the plants which were sent?   .

A. I don't know that he did.

Q. You do not remember that you refused to let him pay for them when he offered to pay?

A. No, sir.

Q. You do not know that he paid Mr. Hall for them?

A. I do not. If he did, Mr. Hall never made any mention of it.

Q. The report of the testimony in the *American* of yesterday states that you said in your testimony here that I gave as a reason why the portions of your report which were eliminated by the board should be eliminated, that such report, if presented to the Legislature, would prevent the appropriation by the Legislature of any money for the hospital?

A. I swear that you said so in the committee. I swear that Governor Bradford was present and John W. McCoy was present. The question was asked you, and you said: "If that report goes in, we will get no appropriation."

Q. I haven't said I did not say so. I admit I did say it. and I think it was true. I wanted to confirm that portion of that testimony. You went on to state, according to that report, that you believed it was impossible to get rid of our sewage properly; and that being so, this was an improper place for the hospital. In addition to that, as I remember your report, you stated that the hospital had already rendered other property in the neighborhood valueless?

A. Yes.

Mr. COMPTON:

I say now to the committee, and I want it distinctly understood, that these were the reasons which prompted me to say if those statements were reported to the Legislature it would justify the Legislature in refusing to make an appropriation, and I think so still.

DR. CONRAD:

I am much obliged to you.

BY DR. THOM:

Q. I would like to know what the character of the plants was?

A. I remember that there were a few cuttings of grapevines, blackberries and flowering plants. I can't tell you the names of them; they were innumerable. I can remember that there were a great variety of roses.

Q. Rose bushes, or slips?

A. They were little cuttings in pots.

Q. Slips, were they?

A. They were in very small pots; suppose they had been grown from slips, I don't know.

Q. You say you assisted in packing them; was this a very large box?

A. I did not assist in packing them up. I say it was done.

Q. Was it a large box?

A. It was a rough case perhaps four feet by two by one foot.

Q. Moved by one man?

A. Oh, yes, sir.

Q. And these flowers were in pots?

A. No, they had been knocked out of the pots, and the pots left.

MR. COMPTON [Reading from the *Sun* of March 20th]:

"Dr. Conrad said he preferred charges against Dr. Broome, assistant physician, which were investigated by the board on the 9th instant, and were not sustained. The charges included harsh and severe treatment of patients, and general insubordination on the part of Dr. Broome. Dr. Conrad declined to make the charges known, as they had not been sustained, and they formed no part of the present case. Dr. Conrad said he was not allowed to be present while the witnesses were examined by the board, and the witnesses were not sworn. Dissatisfied with the manner of the investigation and with the result, he wrote and handed in his resignation; that he had not intended to do so up to that moment."

Mr. Farnandis is more familiar than any member of this committee, probably, with what occurred at the board meeting when what Dr. Conrad relates took place, because he conducted the examination on this point, and, if Mr. Farnandis will question Dr. Conrad upon that particular point. I think he can bring out the facts.

Mr. FARNANDIS:

I am perfectly willing to state my recollection of what occurred, if the committee desire.

By Mr. COMPTON:

Q. [To Dr. Conrad.] Were any reasons given why the witnesses should not be sworn?

A. None whatever. Dr. Broome and myself both agreed that the witnesses should be sworn, but it was ordered otherwise by the board.

Q. Did not Mr. Farnandis say that an oath administered would be merely *pro forma* and of no binding effect?

A. Yes, sir, he did say so.

Q. And did he not in so saying speak for the board, and say that it was the pleasure of the board that if any witnesses desired to be sworn, or you desired to have any particular witnesses sworn, they might be sworn?

A. I understood that to have been said: that any witnesses desiring to be sworn; this was the wording of the remark: "Does any witness desire to be sworn."

Q. In other words, did not the board agree that any witness who desired to be sworn, might be sworn?

A. Yes.

Q. Was any reason assigned by Dr. Farnandis, or any other member of the board, why it was desired by the board that you and Dr. Broome should not be present during the examination?

A. I heard of none.

By GOVERNOR BRADFORD:

Q. Did you express any desire to be present during the session of the board?

A. I did not; but I had a very urgent desire to do so, but was overruled in the first place, and I therefore considered it to be utterly useless to express any such desire, since it was decided that Dr. Broome and myself should not be present at the examination, and we were invited out, and therefore I made no protest against it.

Q. But whether you expressed any desire or not that any particular witness should be examined under oath?

A. No, sir; I did not. I asked that all should be sworn.

By DR. THOM:

Q. Did you not make a proposition to the board that you would discharge the magistrate whom you had caused to be brought there for the purpose of administering oaths?

A. After the board decided that oaths should not be administered, I then discharged him.

Q. Do you remember that the board said you had better keep the magistrate there, if, perchance, there should be a witness who desired to be sworn, or whom you might desire to have sworn?

A. The magistrate was there until a very late hour.

Q. Don't you remember that after that you came in and said that you proposed to send away the magistrate?

A. Yes, sir.

Q. Mr. Farnandis, acting by the request of the board in making the examination, was it not stated then that you had better retain the magistrate, in order to have an opportunity to administer the oath if any particular witness desired to be sworn, or in case you desired to have him sworn?

A. I don't remember exactly, and I do not deny that that may have been the case, but I really did not see the necessity of keeping a magistrate there to swear my own witnesses, when I was not permitted to cross-examine the witnesses on the other side. It was all done by others.

By GOVERNOR BRADFORD:

Q. You have intimated that you sent in your resignation

A. I read the resolutions of the board immediately. They were handed in at the door as soon as I was able to do so.

Q. Did you send in your resignation before you received the resolution which the board had passed censuring you?

A. No, I did not, but that resolution accompanied the resolution that the charges were not sustained. The board subsequently withdrew that vote of censure for the reason that I stated before the board—in consideration of the fact that the president of the board had twice spoken to me concerning the rough and cruel treatment of Dr. Broome about these patients, and had ordered me to transfer Dr. Broome from the female side to the male side of the hospital. In consideration of the fact that the president knew of this, that was one of the foundations upon which the board withdrew the censure.

Q. Was not this the reason that the board withdrew the censure—that you appeared before them afterwards, and asked the withdrawal of the censure?

A. Yes, sir, I made that statement. I said, "In consideration of two facts I ask the withdrawal of the censure: —in consideration of the fact that the president was aware of these abuses of Dr. Broome, and had three times spoken to me about them, and had ordered me to transfer Dr. Broome from the female to the male department. I stated, in consideration of that fact, I asked its withdrawal.

Q. You did ask them to withdraw?

A. Based upon that fact.

Q. You did ask them to withdraw the censure, and the board having received your resignation, and having by a vote accepted it, then agreed that they would withdraw the resolution of censure?

when the board resolved upon that course in not making the examination of witnesses under oath?

A. No, sir.

Q. Will you state at what time during the progress of these proceedings you sent in your resignation?

A. Based upon those two statements, I said, in consideration of these two facts—that the president knew of these

charges. I said. in consideration of his knowing these
things, I had not brought the matter before the board, considering it the duty of the president to have done so, as he
had spoken to me three times about this abuse of Dr.
Broome, and ordered me to transfer him from the female
to the male side of the hospital. That was one of the
reasons. The censure was based upon the statement of
these charges made as far back as eighteen months ago.

Q. You asked the censure to be withdrawn, and it was
withdrawn: is not that the case?

A. No, sir. I asked the board for an interview after my
resignation was sent in. which was granted, and I said,
"Gentlemen, you have passed a vote of censure upon me
based upon a statement in the resolution, that those charges
should have been presented to the board long since, as they
cover a period of eighteen months." That was the second
resolution. I asked that that vote of censure be withdrawn,
based upon the fact that the president knew of these things
long ago, and had spoken to me about them three times,
and had directed me to transfer Dr. Broome from the female
to the male side of the hospital; in consideration of the
president having knowledge of these facts, and that it was
not obligatory upon me to present the charges to the board
before, since the chief officer of the hospital was aware of
them. I asked the withdrawal of the censure and it was done.

Q. You were not in the board, were you, when it was
stated that while the board were willing to withdraw, yet ——

A. No, sir: I only know that that was my reason, based
upon that fact.

By Mr. COMPTON:

Q. After your letter of resignation was handed in, you
made a request to the board, by letter, for an interview, I
believe?

A. Yes, sir.

Q. When you came in the room did you not say, "gentlemen, I have to request of you that you will withdraw the
censure," or words to that effect; and did you not say, "I
never have had a censure passed upon me before, during all

my long connection with the hospital," and did you not appeal to the board upon that ground to withdraw the censure?

A. No, sir; I said all that you have just stated and then said, based upon the fact. I believe I have the resolutions in my pocket which will show that they were based upon the fact. The resolution was based upon the fact that these charges had existed for eighteen months, and they should have been presented before. Is not that so?

MR. COMPTON:

That is so, and I only want to ask you, if you did not make the appeal for the withdrawal of censure upon the ground that you had never before, in your long experience in the hospital, been censured.

THE WITNESS:

You stated upon these grounds?

MR. COMPTON:

Yes, I admit that.

THE WITNESS:

I thank you for that much. Then those were the grounds upon which the resolution was withdrawn, you admit?

MR. COMPTON:

I can tell you that the board were induced to withdraw the resolution of censure, I think, because of your appeal. and I speak in the presence of four members of the board, and they can say whether I report it correctly or not.

THE WITNESS:

That was the basis of my request.

THE CHAIRMAN:

I think the committee would prefer, gentlemen, that you pass from charge to charge. For instance, there are thirteen specifications, and it would be more systematic and we would get through sooner if you would take the first charge and interrogate him upon that, and then proceed to the next and, so on.

BY DR. CHANCELLOR:

Q. You stated that the report of the board would not bear

criticism, inasmuch as it reported that ninety per cent. of the cases of insanity were cured, whereas the statistics showed only thirty per cent. Did you not ask me that I would give you my report?

A. You brought your report out and read it to me. I said, "It is a very valuable report and reads well, and I would like to have that report; it is really a superintendent's report."

Q. Did you not propose to me to buy it from me?

A. "With certain alterations of that report," I said to you, in a jocular manner, "I will buy it from you."

Q. [Reading.] "He made no remark upon this fact, but did state to Dr. Chancellor, that it would not bear criticism."

A. The part that says, "He made no remark," is not correctly reported.

Q. "It would not bear criticism, inasmuch as it reported that ninety per cent. of insane persons could be cured, whereas the percentage as known to all well-informed physicians is only about thirty." I call the attention of the committee to the report on that head just at this point. On page 8th of the annual report of the Board of Managers of the Maryland Hospital for the Insane for 1877, I will read an extract for the purpose of showing upon what I base my calculation. "About two-thirds (515) of the whole number are under the care and management of the guardians of the poor, with no better provision than the county hospitals, from whence, according to the most accurate data, but few (less than seven per cent.) return with mental integrity, while the experience of hospitals shows that from seventy to eighty per cent. of cases of recent origin treated in these institutions are restored to health." I read that to show that I stated from seventy to eighty and not ninety per cent.

THE WITNESS:

Did not your first report say ninety, and did you not subsequently correct it?

DR. CHANCELLOR:

No, sir; I never made any change in it after the report was adopted.

THE WITNESS:

Did you not have Dr. Broome correct it?

DR. CHANCELLOR:

I read the report and asked for corrections. You stated at the time that the per-centage of cured was too great, and so did Dr. Broome. But I propose to show upon what I base my calculation. I will now read from the report of Dr. Conrad for 1876, on page 12th: "The statistics of hospitals for the insane in this country show that at least seventy-five per cent. of cases of recent origin are cured, whilst they also show that but seven per cent. are cured in almshouses." That is your report, isn't it, Doctor?

THE WITNESS:

I will now state that, in 1874, I read an article, based on statistics that I had picked up, which once stood well. Dr. Jarvis reports that ninety per cent. were cured, and I can show you statistics that ninety-nine per cent. are cured. In 1874, I must admit, that I did assert, or write, that ninety per cent. were cured, and I based that statement upon the statistics of Dr. Jarvis. Since that time, having examined this subject more carefully and examined more recent reports—the reports of Dr. Sutherland, of the Commission of Lunacy of Scotland, and Dr. Chapin, based on two hundred and odd thousand cases, and tracing those cases out until their death—these have proved very conclusively that there are but thirty per cent., when I myself stated, three years ago, that ninety were cured, basing my statement on the statistics of Dr. Jarvis. I cannot say exactly what statement I do base this report on.

Q. That is your report?

A. Yes, sir; but it was based on statistics just as this was, and I said to you. "Your report won't bear criticism :" the proportion is changing constantly.

Q. I will ask you one question in regard to the cottage system—did you ever advocate the cottage system?

A. I have, and I do now.

Q. Did you ever advocate it in connection with that hospital?

A. I did, at one time. I advocated it most of the time, and I would advocate it now if the surroundings in regard to water and sewage were such as to justify colonization.

Q. Did we not discuss that matter previous to the presentation of the report?

A. We have talked over the matter; I don't know that we have brought it down to that very question.

Q. Did we not discuss the question as to which would be the best, the addition of another wing to the present hospital, or the introduction of cottages?

A. Yes, sir, we did.

Q. And you concurred with me that the cottages would be best?

A. Yes, sir, and I would like to have cottages there. As I stated at the time, with the laboring patients outside, coming and going, and dirtying the halls, a cottage for those would be very proper indeed.

Q. Did we not walk over the ground and discuss where the proper location for those cottages would be?

A. We did. We have walked over the ground and at the same time discussed the different locations. The executive committee, for instance, discussed the location of the carpenter's shop, and I objected to its being placed there, because it was too remote from the house. It was, nevertheless, placed there, and I had no more to say.

First Charge Read.

THE WITNESS:

I will state that the remarks in quotation marks, "canvassing the individual members of the board for his own appointment as the chief medical officer of the hospital, (salary implied), stating that an officer resident at the hospital could not control the institution in consequence of intimate association with subordinates," are the ones that I propose to summon Dr. Brown to testify upon. He told me so.

THE CHAIRMAN:

We will have him here.

By Dr. THOM:

Q. I would like to ask if in that charge you meant to individualize Dr. Thom?

A. I give this statement in quotation marks, and I give my witness. I, myself, know nothing about that charge farther than what Dr. Thomas Brown has told me. I, therefore, have caused Dr. Brown to be summoned to corroborate that statement in quotation marks.

Second Charge Read.

By Dr. CHANCELLOR:

Q. Do you know what time this occurred?

A. The books will show the transfer; I cannot recollect.

Q. About how long ago?

A. I really can't say. I know the transfer was made at the time Mr. Gunther was away at the springs, I think.

Q. Did you go to Mr. Shawgo and examine his groceries?

A. I was directed by you several times to go there and examine his groceries.

Q. Were you satisfied with them?

A. Yes, sir; he had good groceries.

Q. How did his prices compare with the prices of groceries at other establishments?

A. Very favorably.

Q. Has any complaint been made to you by the steward in regard to certain groceries?

A. No, sir.

Third Charge Read.

By Dr. THOM:

Q. When this thing occurred with regard to the carpets, does that charge have reference to any time when I was a member of that board?

A. I don't think so.

Dr. THOM:

I was not on the board?

THE WITNESS:

I think not. At the time of the attack upon Dr. Chancellor, by the press, I don't think you were a member of the board.

By Dr. CHANCELLOR:

Q. Did you ever make any complaint to the purchasing committee in regard to this matter?

A. I did not.

Q. Did you ever make any complaint to the board?

A. I did not. I made an application to the board to receive my orders through one or more sources, instead of receiving them from so many sources. Whether that source was Dr. Chancellor, or whether it was the secretary, I don't know, but I generally received orders from Dr. Chancellor, and supposed him to have been the source.

Q. Was I not a member of the purchasing committee at that time?

A. No, sir; not that I know of. The purchasing committee was Mr. Gunther and Mr. McSherry.

Q. Do you remember whether Mr. Gunther was in the city at that time?

A. He was not.

Q. Was Mr. McSherry?

A. No, sir.

Q. Could the orders have come through any other member, or could I have conferred with the purchasing committee?

A. Not that I know of; and I knew of no good reason for the change. I had had orders from Mr. Gunther to continue my purchases of carpets from Turnbull & Bro. I must say, that I found, after the transfer to Mr. Griffith, that there was a saving of about ten per cent. over the purchases at Turnbull's. I think Mr. Brown will corroborate the statement that they were cheaper.

By Dr. THOM:

Q. When did you discover that difference between the prices?

A. The discovery was on the purchase of some carpets—a difference of ten cents on the dollar.

Q. Do you remember the purchase of carpets at Turnbull's by Mr. Gunther and myself?

A. I do.

Q. Do you remember what that price was?

A. I do not.

Q. You do not remember that it was ninety cents?

A. I do not, and I am not now referring to that carpet.

Q. I merely wanted to get the difference?

A. I don't remember about it.

BY DR. PERKINS:

Q. You state here that this gentleman stated to you his reason why he refused to give a letter of indorsement of the Doctor's report upon almshouses; can you give us that reason as assigned to you for his refusal to indorse that important document?

A. The gentleman is here, he can speak for himself.

Fourth Charge Read.

BY DR. CHANCELLOR:

Q. Did I state any reason to you why I desired you to make purchases of Mr. Dillehunt?

A. Yes, sir; you told me it would help you through with the ordinance for the transfer of pauper patients from Bayview Asylum to Spring Grove.

Q. How long did you purchase from him?

A. Until you told me to make the transfer back again. I think, also, that I complained to you,

Q. And then I told you, did I not, unhesitatingly to make the change?

A. I complained to you that the prices were higher and that the tobacco was worse.

Q. And I told you, unhesitatingly, to make the change?

THE WITNESS:

Do you remember your remark following it?

DR. CHANCELLOR:

No, sir; I asked you a question.

THE WITNESS:

You remember the others quite well?

DR. CHANCELLOR:

I am simply asking you a question.

A. You are correct; I did tell you that the price was high and the tobacco was bad, and complained to you.

Q. I sanctioned the transfer back then to the former place, when you told me the prices were higher?

By Dr. PERKINS:

Q. What was the other reason assigned?

A. It was not a reason; it was an epithet. I give the Doctor an opportunity to quote it, I don't care to do it.

Fifth Charge Read.

By Dr. CHANCELLOR:

Q. Did I state to you that the amount paid was for myself individually, or for the purposes of the campaign in the twentieth ward?

A. No, sir; you told me it would aid in your election; those were your words—"To aid in my election."

Q. Did you ever hand me any money to aid in my election?

A. Yes, sir; I have contributed every year, and I have contributed to Mr. Gorman's. I have your receipt now, signed by Mr. Gorman.

Q. I sent it to Mr. Gorman, and returned you Mr. Gorman's receipt.

A. Yes, sir, you did. I make it a matter of duty to contribute every year.

Q. Have you purchased anything from Kelly & Piet since I requested you or ordered you to make purchases from Mr. Dulaney?

A. I considered it in the light of an order, and made the purchases in consequence of the order. You did not, generally, give me your orders in a peremptory manner.

Q. Did I not always make requests in regard to these things?

A. Yes, you were not in the habit of giving me peremptory orders for anything.

Q. Have you purchased anything from Kelly & Piet since?

A. No, sir.

Q. Have you purchased anything except from Dulaney?

A. I told Mr. Graham, after receiving this order, to go to Mr. Dulaney?

Q. Have you purchased anything from Mr. Dulaney subsequent to the time that I stopped visiting the hospital on account of the misunderstanding between ourselves?

A. Not to my knowledge. The order to Mr. Graham was to go to Mr. Dulaney. If he has gone elsewhere, I am not conscious of it. If there was anything needed, the order has been for Mr. Graham to go to Mr. Dulaney's, and, if articles have been purchased elsewhere, I am not aware of it.

Q. Are you aware that anything was purchased for the hospital from Mr. Dulaney previous to this time?

A. Not that I am aware of.

Q. You are not aware that I made purchases for the board soon after its organization? Did I not show you some letter-headings that I had purchased from Mr. Dulaney, which you said were very nicely gotten up?

THE WITNESS:

Do you mean concerning the State Board of Health?

DR. CHANCELLOR:

No, sir. The managers of the hospital.

A. I really don't remember.

Q. You remember the usual headings of my official letters for the hospital?

A. Yes, sir.

Q. Do you not remember that you said to me that that was very much nicer than your's, and I told you I got it from Mr. Dulaney?

A. Yes, I think I do.

Q. That was in 1876, soon after the organization of the board, and long prior to the time that this contribution was made to me as a Ward officer and chairman of the Finance Committee?

A. I think the books will show no other purchase to my knowledge, and I had quite forgotten that. I know that I asked Mr. Gunther where I should get the stationery from, and he told me to continue at Kelly & Piet's.

Q. Did you think it was an imperative duty upon you to

do so, when I made the simple request that you should divide the patronage and purchase from Dulaney?

A. You had always given the orders in the form of requests; you had never given peremptory orders, as I have just stated, and I generally complied with your requests. Your orders were given in the shape of requests.

Sixth Charge Read.

BY DR. CHANCELLOR:

Q. How do you know that I purchased them without authority of the committee?

A. I only give it on the authority of Dr. Brown.

Q. How do you know that Dr. Brown knows that? He was not one of the committee.

A. He told me so. The charge stands or falls upon his evidence. The charge is made upon the report of Dr. Brown to me.

Q. You don't know the fact that Mr. Gunther, the other member of the committee, authorized me to make the purchase of the horses?

A. I do not.

Seventh Charge Read.

BY DR. CHANCELLOR:

Q. What repairs were those?

A. The repairs of the bath-room and plumbing, repairing of pipes.

Q. Did you not inform me that these places were leaking and injuring the ceiling and rotting the floors?

A. I informed a number of members In walking around I invariably pointed out the falling of the ceiling to the members of the board, just as I did to you.

Q. Did you not tell me there was an urgent necessity to have that repaired?

A. You asked me, and I said, "Yes."

Q. Are you not aware that Mr. Gunther was the other member of the executive committee; that we had had only the two meetings of the board, at which Mr. Farnandis and Mr. Compton and myself were present; that was in the summer time, you remember, when we could not get a quorum of the board?

A. I remember there were several occasions when there was not a quorum present.

Q. Do you not remember this time?

A. No, I don't remember that.

Q. Do you not remember that Mr. McCoy, the chairman of the committee, was absent from the city a considerable time last summer?

A. Yes, sir; but not at the time these repairs were ordered.

Q. Did you ask me to send a plumber to have repairing done?

A. No, sir, I did not; on the contrary, I said to you after the man had proceeded three days, that that work belonged to the executive committee, and that there might be some disturbance about it. You then went after Mr. McCoy and brought Mr. McCoy out.

DR. CHANCELLOR:

I remember that, and Mr. McCoy sanctioned what I had done.

THE WITNESS:

To the amount of one hundred dollars.

DR. CHANCELLOR:

He sanctioned the entire proceeding.

THE WITNESS:

Dr. McCoy is a witness in this investigation.

Q. Was the work done?

A. Very well done.

Eighth Charge Read.

No one wishing to make any inquiries in regard to this charge, the

Ninth Charge was Read.

BY DR. CHANCELLOR:

Q. Are you aware of the fact—I know you are not personally aware of it—but are you aware from representation, that I have been almost the entire winter confined to my house?

A. No, sir; I have seen mention of your presence at the council meeting, and especially on the night the confirmation of officers took place, and since and before. I remember seeing you on the street frequently, and I heard that you were at Annapolis to visit the Governor.

Tenth Charge Read.

Dr. Chancellor stated that he had no questions to ask.

Eleventh Charge Read.

DR. CHANCELLOR:

I have no questions to ask.

Twelfth Charge Read.

BY DR. CHANCELLOR:

Q. What patient was that?

A. Mrs. Tyler; she was sent out to the hospital. She was a daughter of Mr. Edwards, and had been a patient there before. She resides at Washington, and after having been in Spring Grove Asylum she returned to her husband. He brought her back to the asylum in an insane condition, and deposited her at her father's door while he was in the act of moving, as the father told me. Her father brought her to the hospital, but I refused to admit her, as she had no certificate. I knew that she had been there formerly, and that she was insane, but there were no certificates of the fact, and I objected to receiving her. Her father begged and beseeched me to hold her for a few days, until he could see Dr. Chancellor, and promised me that he would bring out the papers either the next day or the day following. I thought at the time that his promise would not be fulfilled. As soon as Dr. Chancellor came out, in a day or two, I spoke to him concerning the matter, and the Doctor said: "Just let it rest and I will see that it is attended to."

Q. She afterward got a permit from the Health Commissioner?

A. I have never seen it. She is still there without permit, authority or certificates.

DR. CHANCELLOR:

I was not aware of that fact.

THE WITNESS:

I think her father resides in the ninth ward; No. 1600 and something Lexington street. Her husband is a resident of Washington.

Q. Did she have a certificate when she was there first?

A. Yes, sir.

Q. You knew the fact that she was insane?

A. Yes, sir, and had been discharged; but it is the rule, that after they have been absent from two weeks to a month, if they return, they must have new certificates.

Q. Are you aware of the fact that we were threatened with a writ of *habeas corpus* if we removed her from the hospital?

A. Yes, sir.

Q. Are you aware that her husband deserted her in the streets of Baltimore, and that she was picked up by the police?

A. It was on that account that I took her on a promise of her father that he would get me the papers.

BY MR. COMPTON:

Q. The most of these charges you bring against Dr. Chancellor antedate the first of last November, do they not?

A. Yes, sir.

Q. How is it that you wrote in the conclusion of your report, which bears date in November, 1877, the following: "I have also to express my thanks to the Board of Managers for the courtesy that they have always shown and assistance they have cheerfully given to me in the discharge of my own duties?"

A. I say so still, up to the last of November.

Q. You thanked the board?

A. I did.

Q. Is that consistent?

A. I think so. These are things that pertain to the hospital, and not to individuals.

Q. You signed as superintendent of the hospital, I believe: this is your report?

A. Yes, sir.

BY THE CHAIRMAN:

Q. Have you with you that portion of your report which was suppressed?

A. I have.

Q. Will you read it?

THE WITNESS READ AS FOLLOWS:

A large number of chronic, incurable lunatics have, therefore, accumulated from year to year, crowding the wards of those hospitals already built to the exclusion of the recent and curable cases. It is this class, the chronic insane, that now require to be provided for. It is manifestly unwise, as well as unnecessarily expensive, to retain these cases in curative hospitals, and a great wrong to them to be kept in the neglected county almshouses of the State. It becomes a serious question, therefore, what to do with the chronic insane. This question has been settled in the State of New York, where it is much more pressing than elsewhere, by the erection and equipment of a large hospital on the cottage plan for the care and custody of the chronic insane exclusively. This hospital is located on Lake Seneca, and includes in its grounds four hundred and seventy-five acres of land. The plan was considered an unwise one by the Association of Superintendents for the Insane, and a resolution to that effect was passed by that body. Notwithstanding the objection urged, the plan has proven a success, and now affords care for one thousand five hundred insane persons, who would otherwise be ill-treated and cared for in the county almshouses of the State. It is this general plan that I would recommend to be adopted for the care of these unfortunate insane of our own State, whose condition has been so forcibly represented by Dr. Chancellor in his late report to his Excellency. The report shows seven hundred and forty-seven indigent insane in the State, of which number only about two hundred and fifty have any kind of suitable care or treatment. Their condition should receive the earliest possible attention of the State, [expunged portion begins at the quotation marks,] " and ways and means instituted to fulfill that purpose at as early a day as possible. " This can most expeditiously (be) done by building cottages " on the farm at this hospital, or by the purchase of Montview Hospital at Frederick, which, in its construction, is " admirably adapted for the purpose of a chronic lunatic " hospital, and is susceptible of extension on the cottage " plan indefinitely.

" There are some reasons why I would not recommend " the congregation of so large a number of insane on the " farm of the Maryland Hospital, by cottages or otherwise. " The farm contains but one hundred and thirty-six acres " of land, which is a small area (in its present shape) for so " large a population of insane. It is also located in the " midst of and surrounded by country seats, occupied during " the summer season by families, the male members of which " are mostly absent, and the females more or less unpro- " tected from any escaped or trespassing lunatics. Besides, " the adjoining property to the hospital-farm is already im- " paired in value by reason of the presence of the hospital, " and the colonizing of the whole number of insane of the " State on the farm would serve to still further depreciate " their value. It is the duty and interest of the State to " protect rather than degrade the value of individual as well " as respect the private interests of her citizens, when it " may do so without injury to itself. Another and important " inherent objection arises from the difficulty now being felt " in disposing of the sewage of the present population. " This, of course, must be provided for in one way or " another, but at present the prospect of doing so, satisfac- " torily, is so far a problem as to make any further increase " in the quantity of doubtful propriety. The water supply " of the hospital is also very limited, and, in seasons of " drouth, occasions apprehensions of deficiency. It is time " that we have reason to believe, from recent explorations

" made, that the water supply will be abundant, yet the fact
" is not established beyond a doubt, and any risk in this
" important element of every-day life would be but to re-
" peat the error which was made in the original selection
" of the site of the hospital.

" Still another objection to further extending the popula-
" tion of the hospital beyond its original capacity, exists in
" its distance from railroad communication and consequent
" cost of procuring supplies by wagon transportation.

" In consideration of these difficulties, which were not
" foreseen in the beginning, but are now apparent, I do not
" think it would be wise to still further add to them.   The
" Montview Hospital, at Frederick, already contains about
" ninety insane, and is admirably constructed for the pur-
" pose of a chronic hospital for the insane, and is so arranged
" as to be capable of indefinite extension, as necessity may
" require.   It was built at a cost of one hundred and twenty
" thousand dollars, with a capacity for two hundred patients.

" Sewage and Water.

" What to do with the sewage of so large an establish-
" ment, located far into the interior, has been a serious
" question in the management of the hospital.   The loca-
" tion of the building, far remote from any bold stream or
" water course, was a serious mistake among others in the
" selection of the site.   The only stream into which the
" sewage could and has been discharged is one running
" through the farm and having its origin from a number of
" small springs in its own immediate vicinity.   Three of
" these springs are located on the land of the hospital, one
" each on the adjoining property of Mr. Albert and Mr.
" Mathews.   The combined water supply of these springs
" scarcely exceeds twenty thousand gallons in twenty-four
" hours, during the dry summer months, and in seasons of
" drouth the supply is so small as to excite apprehensions
" of scarcity.   The average daily consumption of water ne-
" cessary for the hospital has been found to be twelve thou-
" sand gallons per day.   This amount is taken from the

" stream by means of dams located near the sources of sup-
" ply and a considerable distance above the point where the
" sewage pipe discharge into the stream. The daily hospital
" supply is passed through the hospital and returned again
" through sewage pipes to the stream at a point near the
" line of an adjoining neighbor, through whose property
" the stream combines to pass. It will be seen from the
" description given that the stream (running about twenty
" thousand gallons per day in dry weather) has about three-
" fourths of its volume polluted by sewage, which is suffi-
" cient to render it unfit for any purpose whatever, and also
" render it a nuisance to the property through which it
" passes. In consequence of the nuisance of this stream,
" about three years ago the owners of property injured by
" the pollution of the stream applied to the court for an in-
" junction and assessment of damages, which was compro-
" mised by the President and Board of Vistors by cutting
" off the sewage discharge to the stream and the payment
" of damages amounting to three thousand four hundred
" dollars.

" The water-closets have not since been used, but Moale's
" dry-earth closets were substituted in their places through-
" out the hospital, and have been in operation since the
" summer of 1874.

" It was thought, from the high endorsements which this
" system enjoyed, that with diligent care and attention they
" would supply the necessities of the hospital, and give no
" offence to the wards. This expectation has not been ful-
" filled. Insuperable difficulties exist in their management,
" owing to the class of patients who use them, and as a con-
" sequence, they have proven a nuisance throughout the
" building. Since the water-closets were closed, the stream
" has been purer than before, but not entirely free from ob-
" jection, owing to another cause, which is indispensable
" in its operation, the bath, kitchen and lavatory water,
" amounting to about ten thousand gallons daily, from ne-
" cessity is still discharged into the stream, and is a source
" of pollution to the water, much to the annoyance and dis-

" comfort of neighbors. Although they have been very
" patient in the expectation of relief, we cannot much longer
" tax their indulgence. Indeed, unless a remedy for the evil
" is applied, before the next summer, legal proceedings will
" doubtless be taken to entirely abate the nuisance, which
" has now existed more or less since the occupation of the
" hospital.

" The urgency of the subject was brought to the atten-
" tion of the board soon after their organization, and vari-
" ous plans were devised for the abatement of the nuisance
" and disposition of the sewage. Wells were sunk at con-
" siderable expense, in the hope that they would receive the
" volume of polluted water and dispose of the fluid by
" absorption or otherwise. But it was found that the nature
" of the underlying strata of earth was such as to preclude
" the possibility of this expectation. In order to still further
" test the character of the earth at many different points,
" borings by means of augur was resorted to with no better
" hope of success. In the meantime, several distinguished
" sanitary engineers made careful examination of the situ-
" ation, each one proposing different plans for the correction
" of the evil. The plan of irrigation suggested by Dr.
" Folsom was not considered practicably applicable to the
" case, by reason of the nature and topography of the land
" and proximity to the hospital. That of filtration, by means
" of cisterns, recommended by Dr. Billings, was not found
" so successful in its operations at the Soldiers' Home as to
" justify the outlay in its construction at this hospital. The
" different systems of disposition of sewage involving exten-
" sive machinery and appliances, are costly to begin with,
" doubtful in result, and require an amount of labor and re-
" pair, the annual cost of which would, in course of a few
" years, pay for the discharge of the sewage into the nearest
" point of the Patapsco river by means of terra-cotta pipes.
" This, I fear, may be the dernier resort. The nuisance
" *must* be removed, or the hand of the law will do it for us,
" and probably at an expense that would long since have
" accomplished the object.

" *Heating and Ventilation.*

" The extensive heating apparatus which has heretofore
" supplied heat to the halls of the hospital has not given a
" satisfactory temperature in the remote halls during exces-
" sively cold weather, whilst the immense amount of coal
" consumed and expense attending its operation have been
" very burdensome. The ventilation system connected with
" it has also proven to be only a name for something that
" may be imagined, so far as its efficiency is concerned.

" On account of the imperfections of these important
" elements of health and comfort, as well as the very great
" cost attending them, your attention is called to the neces-
" sity of some radical change being instituted or modifica-
" tion made in the present system of heating and ventilation.
" There are certainly no two essentials to a well appointed
" hospital so paramount in importance as the subject under
" consideration, heat and ventilation, unless possibly sew-
" age and water supply compete for the ascendency as
" factors in the vital statistics, as well as difficulties of ac-
" complishment. The settlement of these grave questions,
" which should have been the first asked and answered,
" before the spade was put into the foundation of the hos-
" pital, you are called upon to confront and adjust. It is
" much more difficult and ultimately expensive to alter and
" adjust an old system to meet modern views and experi-
" ence, than to establish a new system upon advanced prin-
" ciples. The system of heating the different halls and
" wards of a large hospital from one central source of heat
" is an error to begin with. Any break or fault in the source,
" or between it and the main distribution, must deprive the
" entire building of heat, and possibly, too, at a time when
" it may be most needed. The temperature of the hospital
" from such a source is supposed to be equal, which is not
" always to be desired. In one hall or ward a certain tem-
" perature may be desired, whilst a different temperature
" may be needed in another. Then, too, it is seen to result
" from all systems of central source of heat that the most

" remote halls and rooms receive the least supply, and may
" be most exposed to cold and change of temperature. This
" is the case with our apparatus and its supply of heat.

" The reservoirs of heat in all hospitals should be multi-
" plied as often as the peculiar construction of the building
" may require, and have a heat radius or circulation of its
" own independent of any other. In this way a single hall
" or ward, or two of them, may be heated without affect-
" ing the temperature of any other. Should any repairs be
" needed in the apparatus in cases of extreme cold, the hall
" may be temporarily abandoned until the repair is made,
" which cannot be done when there is one central reservoir
" of heat. These principles may be embodied in the sec-
" tional boiler and hot water circulation of different patterns.
" They are automatic in operation and require but little
" labor as compared with the high-pressure apparatus.

" The ventilation, also, may be adapted best to small areas
" than to large. It is manifestly much easier to move a
" small body of air than a large one, and especially so when
" the smaller body has less angler and comparatively less
" friction to contend with than necessarily attaches to the
" movement of a large volume through the diversified
" avenues of a large building. If these combined princi-
" ples of heating and ventilation were observed in large
" public buildings, I am quite sure we would hear less of
" difficulties in heating and ventilation. With heating ap-
" paratus, as with many modern asylums recently built,
" they are too magnificent in proportions, cost too much,
" and then, too, do not yield proportionate results, and some-
" body else must bother their heads to alter the defects,
" change the system, and spend more money on the machine.
" This is just what has recently been done, at a cost of about
" four thousand dollars, with the promise of satisfactory
" temperature and great economy of coal. These two prom-
" ises are yet to be realized in the coming winter.

" It would have been better, if time and means had justi-
" fied so radical a change, to have abandoned the elaborate

" apparatus that we are saddled with and substituted the
" sectional boiler of hot-water circulation. One such reser-
" voir of heat placed under each tier of halls, having a
" circulation limited to them, with direct heat to the halls,
" and indirect supplied to the bed-rooms. This plan, I am
" sure, would give better results than any other, and at less
" expense by one-half. The expense attending the change
" will be compensated for in economy of operation in the
" course of three or four years. The modified apparatus
" which we now have was perhaps the only thing to be done
" at the time, owing to the want of funds and time to ac-
" complish more."

By Dr. THOM:

Q. When did you come to the conclusion set forth in that
part of the report just read by you?

A. It was a matter in my mind some time. I expressed
it to you, I think, some weeks before the meeting at Mr.
William Taylor's, if you remember. You were with Mr.
Taylor at different times.

Dr. THOM:

I remember the occasion.

THE WITNESS:

And Dr. Broome also told me that he had told you.

Q. Do you remember talking with me during the early
part of the fall, in regard to the plan which he recommended to the board, to wit: the cottage system and its
adaptation to the wants of the people and the merits of that
locality?

THE WITNESS:

Where was that conversation?

Q. Were you not at the hospital on one or two occasions,
and did you not on one occasion, after talking and arguing
about it, tell me that you had written a paper which you
would be very glad for me to read, in which you had set
forth those views more fully?

A. Yes, sir.

Q. That recalls the fact of the conversation?

A. Yes, sir.

Q. And this book was furnished by you to me as giving more in detail what you thought on the subject?

A. Yes, sir.

Q. But you do not remember the time when you arrived at a different conclusion?

A. No, I cannot tell you the exact time. It had been a a matter of gradual growth from close observation of these matters; for instance, in September of last year, we had a great deal of apprehension lest our water supply should cease.

Q. Do you remember that before September I never discussed anything about the hospital?

A. Yes, sir.

Q. Therefore, what took place in the line of argument and discussion must have occurred after September?

A. Yes, sir; very likely.

Q. Do you remember the date of that very document which you have just read from—when it was penned?

A. It was not completed at the time of the board-meeting, in the second week of November; I was writing on it that morning.

Q. So that it must have been between the time of my advent to the board and the date of that paper that this discussion between you and myself took place?

A. I cannot tell the time, exactly, when I changed my opinion; it was not a precipitate matter—it was a matter of growth. For instance, the sewage question was determined in my mind by an examination of the building. You know well enough, Mr. Taylor, our neighbor, has suffered very much for water, and last September he sent up to us to send him some water.

Q. That is not the point. I want to get at the time when your mind underwent this violent change?

A. It was not a violent change.

Q. I want to know when your mind changed directly opposite to the views which you expressed to me?

A. There was no violent change in my mind. It was created, as I told you, by observation of many things.

DR. THOM:

The first time that I knew of the change was when your report was read to the board, and if anybody else had given it out I would not have been more astounded. I wish to fix the period when this change came over your mind, when your judgment was altered in the premises.

THE WITNESS:

I do not think I expressed it to anybody else except Dr. Broome, perhaps.

By MR. KNIGHT:

Q. One of your complaints was, that you were hurried by the president and were not allowed time to make your report?

A. I stated that—that the Doctor gave me one week to make the report, and I said: "It is impossible to do it; it is out of the question. We ask for three in order to make out our quarterly report. We usually meet on the second Tuesday of each month, and we found that two weeks was hardly sufficient time to make up accounts and get in the bills, and I asked for three weeks, which was granted." When the annual report came I was granted one week, and said that was impossible, and the Doctor granted two. The Doctor then said: "You must have it done in that time."

By DR. CHANCELLOR:

Q. You are aware that the board fixed the 14th of November as the time when they desired these reports?

A. I think that was the time.

Q. And I stated to you that the board had passed a resolution desiring the reports to be handed in at that time, and that Governor Carroll had requested a synopsis of the reports, in order that he might make up a message from it?

A. Yes, sir; you remember me stating that the law required them to be made in September, and that the Governor could make up his remarks in a much shorter time than I could make up a whole annual report, and the remark, also, that I must have it if it required day and night work.

Q. And I urged you, I believe, if I am not mistaken, to let me have your report, that I might see it previous to writing mine?

A. I don't remember that at all.

Dr. CHANCELLOR:

I frequently asked you in regard to the progress of your report, did I not?

THE WITNESS:

What particular portion of the report?

Dr. CHANCELLOR:

I wanted to know your views on several matters, especially in regard to the water supply and cottage system.

THE WITNESS:

I don't think you ever consulted me in regard to the water supply.

Q. You are aware of the fact that Dr. Ames visited the hospital, and we had a long conversation in regard to that?

A. Yes, sir, I do: it was very near the time of the report.

Dr. CHANCELLOR:

There are two paragraphs in my report I would like to have read, if it will be permissible, simply to ask the Doctor if he suggested any change.

Dr. CHANCELLOR read as follows:

" To increase the capacity of the hospital by adding wings to the present building would possess some advantages in an economical point of view, but not commensurate with the advantages to be realized in the cottage system. If the State wishes to provide properly for the cure of its insane citizens, the cottage plan will undoubtedly be found the best: but what is *best* to be done, and what can be done, are two very different propositions, the decision of which must rest with the Legislature, bearing in mind the imperative necessity for increased accommodations. The cost of the cottages may be approximated by reference to the letter of J. Crawford Neilson, Esq., architect, which is presented with this report.

" It would simplify the question of providing for the future increase of the insane if local almshouses and workhouses combined were established by a union of counties, where idiots, imbeciles and dements could be amply cared for and made to contribute, by their physical labor, to their own care and maintenance."

Q. Did you suggest any change here when I read you my report?

A. No, sir; I considered that I had no right whatever to change your report. I had no right to object to your report at all, and I considered that you had no right, under the by-laws, which I propose to read, to object to my report.

DR. CHANCELLOR:

I never claimed the right to object.

THE WITNESS:

Under the head of "Duties of the Superintendent and Treasurer," the by-laws say: "At which annual meeting of the board he shall present a *tabular view* of the institution for the year, with full and minute details from the records, and accompanying it with a condensed report of other interesting and useful facts and circumstances, experiments and opinions, illustrating its management, conditions and prospects."

By DR. PERKINS:

Q. Who suppressed the portion of your report which you have read?

A. A committee appointed by the Board of Managers (Mr. Compton, Mr. Bradford, and Mr. McCoy) to confer with me concerning this difference of opinion in regard to the report.

Q. Was that suppressed by an order of the State Board, or by a committee of the board?

A. It requested, or demanded, I really cannot tell which, its withdrawal.

By MR. COMPTON:

Q. When and where?

A. At the hospital. Mr. Compton was chairman of that committee, and Mr. McCoy and Mr. Bradford were the other members.

Q. Your report was read by the board and criticised by the board, was it not?

A. I don't know; I was not present.

Q. You knew the fact that your report was referred to the committee composed of myself, Mr. McCoy, and Governor Bradford?

A. I was informed of it.

.Q. I informed you, did I not?

A. Yes, sir.

Q. Do you not remember that before the committee and board left the hospital that afternoon you came to me and asked me to allow you to have the report?

THE WITNESS:

That portion of it which was withdrawn?

Mr. COMPTON:

No, sir: the whole report.

A. I don't really remember that.

Q. Don't you remember that, on that afternoon you came to me and requested me to let you have your report until the following Wednesday?

A. I think I did, because I stated that it was handed in unfinished.

Q. When you handed that report in to me on the following Wednesday, had you not retained that portion of the report which you now say was expunged?

A. I say that I was requested to withdraw this portion of the report that is marked, and I say that I had no knowledge of your desire for its withdrawal until requested to do so by that committee.

Q. Is that your answer to my question?

A. That is my answer.

Q. My question is this—whether on that afternoon you did not ask me to allow you to have your report until the following Wednesday, promising to send it to me, and that when you forwarded it to me it was minus the part which you now hold in your hand?

A. I really could not tell you that; I really do not know; but I do know that that committee requested this portion of my report to be withdrawn which is specified by lead pencil marks.

BY THE CHAIRMAN:

Q. Who put these marks on it?

A. It was done by the committee.

BY MR. COMPTON:

Q. How do you know it was done by the committee?

A. It was handed to me by Mr. McCoy, who stated that that was the objectionable part; that if I would turn over I would see some marks. No, I think it was Governor Bradford who told me that; one or the other handed it to me. I have a faint recollection of asking you to let me have my report.

Q. Don't you remember that you forwarded it to me afterwards, on the following Wednesday, with that part out?

THE WITNESS:

Was that after the committee met?

MR. COMPTON:

Your report was submitted to the board, considered by it, and referred to a committee of which I was chairman. As I left the room, going to the door, you called me and asked me to allow you to have your report until the following Wednesday.

THE WITNESS.

Now I remember it, perfectly. I had another fact in my mind.

Q. Now, I ask you if you don't remember the additional fact that when you returned your report to me, on the following Wednesday, you retained the part that you have in your hand?

A. At the request of the committee, I did.

Q. Not at my request?

THE WITNESS:

I asked you to allow me to have this in order to make the connecting link between the expunged part and the other. I referred to another matter at first, but I remember it perfectly now.

BY DR. PERKINS:

Q. You state, on oath, that the committee condemned that portion?

A. I do, and I was ordered to withdraw it. I then asked
Mr. Compton to let me have it, in order to make the connection intelligently and wind up the report. The committee had requested it, and I took out those objectionable
parts at their request.

BY THE CHAIRMAN:

Q. You stated here, yesterday, that the Board of Visitors
had paid about thirty-four hundred dollars damages; to
whom was that amount paid?

A. The records of the old Board of Visitors will show
the pollution of this stream which it was claimed damaged
Mr. Early's place especially. He had it for sale as well as
I remember, and he was one of those who had damages to
lay against the hospital. I think Mr. Cooper and Mr. Taylor had some wells dug; that was when a previous board
was in existence.

Q. Wasn't there a suit for damages last year?

A. There was, by Mr. Metz, who got three hundred dollars and something; that was under the present Board of
Managers.

Q. How long have you been superintendent of the hospital?

A. Since July, 1876.

Q. These observations and experiences of yours, which
you have collected in your report, have been gathered during that time, have they?

THE WITNESS:

You mean referring to this particular matter?

THE CHAIRMAN:

Yes, referring to sewerage, the water supply, location, &c.

A. I must say that, in 1876, perhaps I would have consented to the introduction of the cottage system. In fact, I
thought so at that time, I had not brought my attention
closely to this matter of sewerage and water supply until
comparatively recently it became a grave question. Even
in the month of September last year I expressed the opinion
that if the water in the pond got lower than it was at that

time—it was then about eighteen inches below the surface—there had better be a conference on the subject with the executive committee or with Dr. Chancellor in regard to sinking some wells at once.

Q. From your experience at that institution you consider it safe, in regard to the supply of water there, to increase the population?

A. In regard to the water, borings have been made recently which show, I think, that water could be obtained, but it is a problem; it is not a settled matter at all; and as a consequence I would not lay a brick on the place until the essential matter of water and essential matter of sewerage should be established beyond any question. I recommended the board to take the sewerage by terra-cotta pipes to the Patapsco below the Relay House, and the cost I do not think would have been as much as by the other line.

I will state, Dr. Folsom, that the Secretary of the State Board of Health of Massachusetts, who has studied sanitary subjects in this country and Europe as a specialty, and perhaps there is no man better informed on these subjects than he is, visited our hospital, and suggested a plan of irrigation, but I thought it was Utopian to irrigate the farm by means of ditches to take out the offensive odors. Dr. Billings also visited the hospital at the request of some of the members. Dr. Billings is of the Johns Hopkins University. He suggested a similar plan, which he had adopted at the Soldiers' Home Hospital at Washington, and I went over there to see the plan. I saw there the system of filtration. The sewerage is passed through several filters sunk in the ground, made of porous brick, and it passes out and is discharged on the surface of the land. When I got there I found it was no service to the ground at all, but the sewerage had backed up and filled the pipes. I went to the point of discharge, and found it to be about as foul as ours is there. Then the plan of Dr. Ames, which has been suggested. I talked with Dr. Ames, and invited him to come out on a Sunday, so that I could with him carefully on this very plan which he suggests in the report. I asked him a great many questions concerning it. My mind was not satisfied.

Q. And is not satisfied now?

A. It is not now. He proposes, after his extensive plan of machinery has failed, if it should fail, or if it accomplishes any one of the purposes—he then proposes to run that water, in the same manner exactly that it is now run at the Soldiers' Home in Washington, through a system of filtration, and then discharge it by means of terra cotta pipes, which in itself is an acknowledgment of a failure of his plan.

G. S. Griffith sworn and examined.

BY THE CHAIRMAN:

Q. Do you know Dr. Conrad.

A. Very well.

Q. Do you know Dr. Chancellor?

A. Very well. I have been acquainted with both those gentlemen for several years.

Q. Did either of them, at any time, buy any carpets from you for the Maryland Hospital for the Insane? If so, when?

A. Dr. Chancellor has purchased goods at my store.

Q. What time did he buy last?

A. I have a little memorandum, prepared by my book-keeper, from which I see that the last account was of purchases made at different dates from August 10th to October 5th, 1870, amounting to one hundred and seventy-four dollars and forty-five cents, as it stands upon the book.

Q. Do you remember Dr. Chancellor calling upon you to endorse his report of the almshouse of the State?

A. Yes; he called upon me soon after his report was published. I think he called at least three times to see me, soon after his report was out. The first time he came he handed me a copy of the report, and we sat down and discussed it somewhat. I think that was just previous to its being sent to the press; the Doctor called again a short time after that. I do not know whether it was the second or third visit he made, but it was after the publications appeared of the County Commissioners, Superintendent of Almshouses, &c. We discussed the merits of the report at that time, and he asked me to give him a letter endorsing his report. I hesitated about it, and told the Doctor that I could not do that: that I thought it should stand upon its own merits: that I had a report which contained a brief account of my visit to the county jails and the almshouses, and if that should be of any service to him he was welcome to it.

Q. Were there any carpets bought for the use of the hospital after that conversation?

A. The report was dated from the 6th to the 10th of July, I think; I do not remember exactly what time it was published—perhaps the last of July. Since that time, as I remarked before, there have been purchases at the establishment from August 10th to October 5th, 1877, amounting to one hundred and seventy-four dollars and forty-five cents.

Q. Have they dealt with you since October?

A. No, sir.

Q. Have you visited all those almshouses and jails?

A. Yes, sir: I have visited the jail and almshouses very frequently for a good many years.

Q. Do you mean all of them, or only a part?

A. All of them.

Q. That was the object of the Doctor's visit—to consult with you because you had had that experience?

A. I presume it was. I had visited those institutions, and am perfectly familiar with the buildings, arrangement, &c.

BY SENATOR STUMP:

Q. Had you shown Dr. Chancellor any favor by reason of which you acquired the custom of the asylum?

A. No, sir: in no way. I never solicited Dr. Chancellor nor Dr. Conrad, in any way.

Q. He subsequently declined to deal with you from the fact of your not having endorsed his report?

A. I have no knowledge of the cause of the stoppage. The first intimations that I had are what appeared in the paper yesterday or to-day.

5

By Dr. PERKINS:

Q. Will you be kind enough to give us your reason for declining to endorse the report of Dr. Chancellor in regard to almshouses?

WITNESS:

Is that pertinent?

[Doctor Perkins insisted upon an answer to the question, and desired the ruling of the committee as to whether it should be answered.]

Dr. PERKINS:

As a foundation for that question, I will state that Dr. Conrad has raised a question here as to the integrity of Dr. Chancellor in certain matters, and assigns as one reason for questioning his integrity, that Dr. Chancellor went to this witness and asked him to endorse his report, which the witness declined to do. If the integrity of Dr. Chancellor is to be dealt with, we want to know the reason for this declination on the part of Mr. Griffith, and I consider the question entirely pertinent.

[The chairman put the question to the committee as to whether the witness should be required to answer the question, and it was decided in the affirmative—five ayes to three noes, as follows:—*ayes*. Messrs. Bannon, Cooper, Acton, Sander and Perkins: *noes*, Messrs. Stump, Knight and Houston.]

[The question was then repeated to witness.]

Dr. PERKINS:

I will explain just here, that if there is any personal reason in regard to the relationship between Dr. Chancellor and the witness, I do not care to press the question; but if it is a question touching a difference of judgment between those two gentlemen, both having visited those institutions and drawn different inferences therefrom, I want an answer.

A. Persons' views may differ after an examination and inspection of such institutions as jails, almshouses, &c., and, as I stated to the Doctor, my views did not correspond in all particulars with his as set forth in the report. I stated to him that I thought he used a good deal of coloring to his statements in some particulars; that in my report I just gave facts; the facts were bad enough, doubtless. Then he spoke in regard to some of the almshouses which he regarded as the worst; for instance, at Hagerstown. I differed from him on that point, about its being the worst, and pointed out to him some of the worst managed houses, including buildings, sanitary arrangements, &c. I think he went to the Hagerstown almshouse at about 8.30 o'clock in the morning, as I understood, before they had time to clean up. Some of the insane have no more moral sense of decency and cleanliness than an animal. You might go to any institution before it had a cleaning in the morning, and I think you would find persons in the condition the Doctor described, which of course gave it the worst effect. If the Doctor had stated in his report that he went there in the morning before the superintendent and others had had time to clean and fit it up, that would have been all right and proper. Then in regard to his description of the building. He states that the jail building at Frederick is a two-story, while it is a three-story building; the one at Cumberland he stated to be a two-story building, while it is a three-story. I am familiar with both of those buildings and the architect of both.

Q. You took the opposite view from what the Doctor expressed in his report in regard to the conditions and general management of the places that had been visited by you both?

A. Yes, sir. Of course different persons see things in different lights.

Q. Can you furnish any one of your reports?

A. Not now; this was a report published some time ago.

S. Thomas Brown sworn and examined.

By THE CHAIRMAN:

Q. You are the steward at the Maryland Hospital for the Insane, are you?

A. Yes, sir.

Second Charge Read.

Q. What is your duty as steward?

A. To make purchases to a certain extent.

Q. You made purchases under the direction of whom?

A. Under the direction of the purchasing committee.

Q. Do you remember any transfer of the purchase of groceries from one house to another? If so, state what you know about it?

A. We had been buying part of the groceries from Stump & Sons—such as sugar, pepper, mustard, and starch. I complained to Doctor Conrad about the pepper, mustard and starch not being what we ordered, and I had to send it back. I do not remember how many times, but I have sent back several boxes. I also complained to Dr. Chancellor about it. Dr. Conrad said he would see about it. He did not say whom he would see. Sometime afterwards, Dr. Conrad told me to go and see Mr. Shawgo. I did not get any orders from anybody else, because Mr. Gunther was not in town at that time; that is to the best of my remembrance. Mr. Gunther was on the purchasing committee at that time.

By Dr. CONRAD:

Q. Do you remember that I told you on one occasion that I had been directed by Dr. Chancellor to purchase groceries at Shawgo's; that I had been to see Shawgo's groceries at the Doctor's request, and that I told you that Dr. Chancellor would like you, also, to go there and look at his groceries, and I think you did so?

A. Yes, I did go.

Dr. CONRAD:

Nothing more was said about the matter, to my knowledge, until you subsequently said to me that the Doctor had directed you to make purchases at Shawgo's.

WITNESS:

I do not remember saying to you that the Doctor had directed me. I do not remember Dr. Chancellor ever telling me to buy any goods. I got my instructions in such matters from you. Dr. Chancellor did request me to buy some little things, such as cheese and crackers, at Shawgo's, which I had been in the habit of buying where I pleased. He said if it was convenient for me, to buy them at Shawgo's; he did not order me to do so.

Q. Did he direct you to employ his colored servant in one of the wards?

A. I asked Dr. Chancellor to send out a waiter.

Q. Did you not say to him that you preferred Jerry, as being better, but that the Doctor had ordered you to employ his man Sam?

A. I remember saying that I did not like Sam.

Q. Did you not say that you did like Jerry, and that Sam was accused of carrying wines, after dinners, down to some persons, and that he broke glasses?

A. I said I did not like this man Sam. I did not say that I saw him carrying things away. That was told to me.

Q. Did you not say to me that you preferred to have Jerry?

A. No, I do not remember of it. I said I did not like Sam.

Q. You had no objection to Jerry, had you?

A. Oh, no.

By Dr. CHANCELLOR:

Q. Did you ever tell me that you did not like Sam?

A. No, sir: I simply asked you to send out a man.

Q. Did you not ask me at the same time to send out a certain amount of oysters by that waiter?

A. I did.

Q. Were you in the habit of getting oysters from Contee's?

A. We had made a contract for the hospital.

By Dr. CONRAD:

Q. Did you not tell me that those oysters cost more, and were not as good as oysters from Contee's?

A. No, I did not say they were not as good—they were better. We paid more for them. I asked Doctor Chancellor to send them out.

BY THE CHAIRMAN:

Q. Are you still employed at the hospital?

A. Yes, sir.

Q. What salary do you receive?

A. Seven hundred dollars a year.

Q. Dr. Conrad is there no more?

A. No, he has not been there for nearly a week.

Q. Dr. Chancellor is President of the Board of Trustees, is he not?

A. I believe so.

William J. C. Dulaney sworn and examined.

BY THE CHAIRMAN:

Q. What is your business?

A. I am in the book and stationery business.

Q. Do you know Dr. Conrad?

A. I do not.

Q. Do you know Dr. Chancellor?

A. I do.

Q. Do you ever sell any articles of stationery to Dr. Chancellor?

A. I have.

Q. Have you at any time aided him in his political career by subscribing any sum of money therefor?

A. Not directly.

Q. Have you indirectly?

A. I have contributed to the twentieth ward fund. He and I happened to reside in that ward, and he has been a candidate several times since we have both resided there, and indirectly I have assisted him.

Q. Would you have contributed the amount you did if he had not been a customer of yours?

A. When I say he has been a customer, I mean that he has been so to such a limited extent that I could hardly recognize him as such. He has bought from me to a very limited degree indeed. I presume Dr. Chancellor has never bought in excess of ten dollars worth, possibly not five dollars worth. He was simply a customer because he has dealt with me.

Q. Did Spring Grove Hospital deal with you to any amount?

A. Yes, sir, they have.

Q. What has been the range of their dealings with you ever since they have dealt with you?

A. From ninety to one hundred dollars.

Q. Then you gave all that away?

A. No, sir, I gave none of that away. What I gave to the twentieth ward fund I gave individually; as a bookseller I did not give anything away. I will state in that connection that I have never been solicited by Dr. Chancellor, and never by any other member of the twentieth ward, though I have resided there seven or eight years. I have always voluntarily contributed. When I have done so I did not contribute for the benefit of any individual, and it was not so understood in any way, shape or form, but to aid a good cause, and I did it unsolicited. The amount contributed voluntarily by me was one hundred dollars, and I happened to give it to Dr. Chancellor because that year he happened to be the treasurer of the board, and it was necessary for me to put it in his hands. I spoke to one other person about it, and he told me that Dr. Chancellor was the person to whom I must hand it over.

By DR. CHANCELLOR:

Q. Did you ever contribute to the twentieth ward when Dr. Chancellor was not the person to receive it?

A. I have, and for a similar amount, and I expect to do so again for as large amount as I can afford.

James H. Shawgo, sworn and examined.

By THE CHAIRMAN:

Q. What is your calling?

A. I am in the grocery business at present.

Q. Where do you live?

A. I live in the twentieth ward.

Q. Do you sell any groceries to the Spring Grove Hospital?

A. Not at present.

Q. Have you sold any?

A. Yes, sir, I have.

By Dr. CHANCELLOR:

Q. The charge is that I changed the purchase of groceries to a man in the twentieth ward, and the implication is, I suppose, that I did it for political purposes. Did I ever speak to you on the subject of politics in any way, shape, or form?

A. Never, sir, since I have been there. It is a remarkable fact that a gentleman so well known in politics has never mentioned politics to me since I have been there.

Q. Who examined those groceries with reference to purchasing?

A. Dr. Conrad examined them at first.

Q. What opinion did he express in regard to them?

A. I remember his saying that the groceries were sold at lower prices and more reasonably.

Q. Did Mr. Brown ever tell you that I sent him there to get groceries?

A. He never told me so.

Q. Did I ever speak to you in reference to the matter?

A. No, sir; not after you spoke to Dr. Conrad.

By Dr. PERKINS:

Q. You are one of the Doctor's constituents, are you?

A. I will let you find that out. I will state that, although I am anxious to testify to the truth in Dr. Chancellor's behalf, I do so in vindication of myself also.

On motion of Senator Stump, the committee adjourned to 9 o'clock A. M., to-morrow, March 21, 1878.

MARCH 21, 1878.

The committee met pursuant to adjournment, Senator Bannon in the chair; present, a quorum.

Doctor Thomas R. Brown sworn and examined.

First Charge Read.

BY DR. CONRAD:

Q. Did you not tell me that Dr. Chancellor canvassed the individual members of the board (with the exception of yourself) " for his own appointment as the chief medical officer of the hospital (salary implied), stating that an officer resident at the hospital could not control the institution, in consequence of intimate association with subordinates?"

A. I have tried, Mr. Chairman and gentlemen, since that charge came to my knowledge yesterday, to refresh my memory and to review every single conversation that I have ever had with Dr. Conrad, and I cannot for the life of me recollect any such statement. I have thought this morning and I thought yesterday—indeed, it occupied my attention a large part of the day—with reference to that one question. I observed, if I mistake not, that a part of the charge contained quotation marks. I would like to say that Dr. Chancellor has never once, directly or indirectly, conversed with me upon the subject. In the first place, I can say that gentlemen have said this to me, knowing my connection with the organization—" What can be Dr. Chancellor's aim in accepting a membership of this board?" and they have said that " he has some ulterior object to gain some position." I have almost uniformly stated that the present law of the institution absolutely prevented Dr. Chancellor, so long as he was a member of the board, receiving any position of emolument. The law provides that members of the Board of Managers shall serve without pay. That any such statement was made by me I would not be willing, under any circumstances, to deny positively. I only state that I have no recollection of any such conversation. I have a recollection of this, and I suppose that I ought to state it, though

I have some question about the propriety of it—that Dr.
Chancellor had observed to one of the members of the
board, on one occasion, that he doubted very much whether
the efficiency of an institution could be maintained if the
head of the institution was in familiar contact with all its
employees: that, to a certain extent, the tone and vigor of
a man's authority were lessened by the fact of constant association.   I have a very distinct recollection of a member
of the board saying that Dr. Chancellor said that to him.
But so far as Dr. Chancellor's interview with me was concerned, I would like to say again that I went one night to
Dr. Thom's house, in the capacity of a pacificator, at the
time these controversies were exciting our great anxiety,
for we were all deeply interested in this question, and believed it could not do anything but injury to the institution.
I went there with the hope that I might be able to break
down the barriers between two gentlemen, who had been,
up to that time, very warm friends.   At that house, Dr.
Conrad, after a number of comments and remarks made,
said—" Dr. Brown, Dr. Chancellor has stated to me "—if I
mistake not, the statement was made in the presence of
some one, but who I cannot remember—" that he intended
to get rid of objectionable men on the board: that there
were certain men on the board that were objectionable to
him and hostile to him, and for that purpose he had consulted with Mr. Gorman with reference to the preparation
of a bill which had for its purpose the ejection of those objectionable men."   If any remark was made, it must have
been made after that time, for I confess I have no hesitation
in saying that I was extremely indignant at the time, if such
was true.   My obvious course was to see Dr. Chancellor
and ask him in regard to that question.   But I saw him by
accident at Dr. McCoy's office.   Dr. Chancellor's object
there was to see if he could not get us all upon a friendly
footing, and stated, in reply to a question of mine, after
some general conversation, that he had never entertained
the prospect or looked to the object which Dr. Conrad had
stated he had, and, in fact, he denied any connection with

this whole question. Whether I repeated, at that time or subsequently, to Dr. Conrad this statement, which had been made to me, I do not know, but I said to myself—"Here comes up this question, and the question has been asked me why Dr. Chancellor is on the board," and I said—"there is nothing that he can accomplish by being on the board, because the law provides that no compensation shall be paid." It is possible that I may have made use of just that statement, that a member of the board had said to me that an individual could not maintain his authority when he was in daily contact with his employees.

BY THE CHAIRMAN:

Q. What time was that conversation—before the legislature met, or since?

A. I am almost sure it was before.

BY DR. CONRAD:

Q. Did you not tell me that you met Dr. Thom on the street one night and had a conversation with him in regard to this very question, and did you not tell me that you said to Dr. Thom—and became quite excited at the same time in that conversation—"If I were perfectly clear in my own mind with regard to the intentions of Dr. Chancellor" (referring to this very matter) "my conduct might be different?" Did you not tell me that you had that conversation with Dr. Thom?

A. No, I never met him on the street one night. I met him one afternoon when he jumped from his carriage. That was previous to this legislation in regard to this proposed reconstruction of the board.

Q. Did you say to Dr. Thom, at that time, that if you were satisfied of the honorable intentions of Dr. Chancellor (or words to that effect) in this matter, your action might be different?

A. Will you explain that question?

Q. I mean referring to this very charge, No. 1: that you held in your mind the opinion that this was more or less so, and having that opinion in your mind, you said to Dr. Thom that night (so you told me) that if you were perfectly satisfied of the honorable intentions of Dr. Chancellor in this matter, your action might be different?

A. It was not at night.

Q. I understood you to say that you had a conversation with him walking along the street at night, in which you said that if you were satisfied of his honorable intentions your action might be different.

A. I do not recall that to mind: I have no recollection of it.

Q. Don't you remember telling me that in your office the very evening after you had met Dr. Thom—don't you remember telling me that you became quite excited and lost your temper?

A. I have no hesitation in saying that I lost my temper, and the reason I lost my temper was the discovery that you made (if it was a discovery) that Dr. Chancellor was making arrangements to legislate me out of the board. It irritated me very much indeed, and I got up to Dr. Thom's house that night and made a remark substantially to this effect: "That is the worst thing yet that has been revealed to me," because it occurred to me that there was no warrant for it. Even if there had been a warrant, I remarked that it was unhandsome for a member of the board to so conduct himself with reference to another member of the board.

Q. Was not this conversation previous to the conversation with Dr. Thom at his house?

A. I cannot positively say: my impression is that it was.

Q. Therefore it could not not have been that conversation which impressed your mind in that direction? Up to that time you had heard nothing from me on that subject?

A. Not a word.

Q. Do you know of any charges against me at the hospital at the time of my resignation?

A. No, sir.

Q. Could you state to this committee whether my administration at the hospital, in all respects, was satisfactory to you so far as you know?

A. As far as I know, you were a very faithful and very

efficient officer. I suppose, Mr. Chairman, if that answer should stand thus, without any qualification, it would perhaps carry a little more with it than I would be willing to be responsible for.

Q. It is your opinion, that is all?

A. When a man gives an estimate of another man, of course he wants that estimate to carry the qualifications with it. I have no hesitation in saying that Dr. Conrad was a faithful, honest, and efficient officer. I have no hesitation in saying, at the same time, that I felt myself called upon in the exercise of a discretion which properly belonged to me in matters of that kind, to believe that Dr. Conrad's fidelity and efficiency did not necessarily conflict with his withdrawal.

Q. Please confine yourself to answers to my questions, as you are now on cross-examination. One other question: Didn't you and Governor Bradford examine the central building and the unoccupied ward and hall, and state that there was sufficient room there still for many more patients, and that as a consequence you could not in your own mind approve the application for other buildings?

A. I don't remember whether Governor Bradford went with me or not. The law provides, however, for an alphabetical visitation of the institution, and from the fact of both our names beginning with B, we may have been there together and made a joint inspection of the hospital. I know we did so on one occasion, and after our visit of inspection had taken place I wanted to make myself familiar with the central part of the building and see what amount of room we had there, and in doing so I found a good deal—how much I would not be prepared to say—of room unoccupied; if I mistake not, an entire hall. I don't think that Governor Bradford went up with me, though I am not sure about it myself. I remember going up and looking at the place, and I found there what I supposed would be room enough for about twenty-five more people, and if I did not say so, it was my opinion that until we had filled up all the space of the hospital there would not be any use in asking for more money to increase its capacity.

Sixth Charge Read.

BY DR. CONRAD:

Q. Did you not say to me that Dr. Chancellor had purchased two horses of a man living in his own ward, and that they were represented to you by another man as being not what they should have been?

A. I would not like to answer the question without an explanation.

Q. I ask you that categorical question.

A. There is a man living in Baltimore—a stable dealer. by the name of Scott. I went to buy a horse from this man Scott, and when I got through with my business he said to me. "You are a pretty lot of men out there at Spring Grove Hospital," or words to that effect; "you have allowed Dr. Chancellor to go to work and buy a pair of horses at a fabulous price, one of which is ringboned"—or spavined, or some other equestrian defect, I do not know exactly what—" and he has done so for the purpose of returning his kindness to him in supporting him," or something of that kind. I made no comment upon it. I said, "Are you certain of that?" He said "I am." My recollection is that I never made any remark to him, but it occurred to me that this would be a great piece of scandal in the community if such things went on, and it is my place to inquire about it. The very next morning I went out to the hospital and went to Dr. Conrad. I did not intimate to him at the time the source of my information, but simply said to him, "Has Dr. Chancellor sent a couple of horses here?" He said, "Yes." Said I, "What is the condition of those horses?" He said, "very good." Then I felt that I would explain why I inquired, and I suppose I told him, though I am not sure of this. I felt perfectly satisfied in my own mind that no wrong had been done; that it was an idle rumor; but I felt at the same time that it was my duty, as a member of the board, to inquire into it. Dr. Conrad's reply to me was that the horses were very good, and I never dreamed until the other day, when I saw this charge, that they were anything different. It had been entirely out of my mind. I do not suppose I had mentioned it from that day to this to any one.

Q. Did you not tell me that Dr. Chancellor had purchased two horses without authority of the committee from a person in his own ward?

A. I have no recollection whatever of making reference to the authority or the absence of authority.

Q. Did you know of it then as a member of the board?

A. I did not, and I do not think, Mr. Chairman, that I was expected to know that. I am a member of the executive committee. The Board of Managers is subdivided into three committees, the finance committee, the purchasing committee and the executive, and the prerogatives of each are quite distinct from those of the other. Our province as members of the executive committee is not to buy cattle, horses, &c. We have other business to attend to. I do not remember making reference to the question of authority at all.

Q. Had you, as a member of the executive committee, known anything about or consulted with any one in reference to the repairs to the water-closets and bath-tubs which had been going on, or which were inaugurated by Dr. Chancellor, as a member of the executive committee, having that particular work in hand (Dr. McCoy, chairman). Had you anything to do at all with that work done under the direction of Dr. Chancellor?

A. I don't remember that the executive committee ever had submitted to them any account of work done in the water-closets, but there has been some work in the repair of pipes reported to me by Mr. McCoy, who is my colleague on the committee.

Q. I mean bath-tubs.

A. I don't remember. I didn't know they had been repaired.

By Dr. CHANCELLOR:

Q. Did this man Scott, the horse dealer, tell you that he had brought two pair of horses to me and tried to sell them to me, but I declined to buy them, because they were defective?

A. No: he did not mention a word to me about that.

Dr. CHANCELLOR:

That is the fact.

THE WITNESS:

My recollection is, since you mention it to me, that he did say to me that he had been trying to sell a pair of horses. To tell the truth, the whole thing is out of my mind. I felt perfectly satisfied that the horses were good ones, and Dr. Conrad himself was my authority for the statement that they were, and that they served their purposes.

BY THE CHAIRMAN:

Q. You stated that there was a good deal of vacant space in the building yet?

A. Yes, to the extent. at the time of our visit, of accommodating, I suppose, about twenty-five more people; but Dr. Conrad would know the space and know the capacity better than I. I counted the rooms, and I must confess that, I was not a little surprised to find so much room unoccupied. Whether that room has been filled up since, I cannot say. because I have not regularly and officially inspected it since that time. That was this last Fall, and there were, at that time, about two hundred and ninty-eight patients in the house, but the number has been increased since that time. If I mistake not, I visited that part of the house last Sunday a week, and it is not filled yet, because one room that was taken at that time is used for a sewing room.

BY Dr. THOM:

Q. Have you ever heard any member of the board, or anybody else, state specifically, prior to the evening, which you cite as having been passed at my house, that Dr. Chancellor proposed to institute proceedings by which certain members of that board would be gotten rid of? Had you ever heard that specific charge made before you heard it at my house?

A. I never heard or dreamed of it before that night.

Q. And that was made by whom?

A. By Dr. Conrad.

Q. So that Dr. Conrad, then, was your informant, with

regard to this matter, which he cites you to prove as having being told him?

A. He was the individual who first informed me on that subject that night. Then the very next morning I met Mr. McCoy, and I said to him, "This is a very curious proceeding we are in the midst of here." I supposed, and I think it was pretty generally the sentiment of the board, that the board had been a harmonious organization, and when this thing came upon me, I was perfectly aghast. He said that Dr. Chancellor had told him that he intended to have a law passed, creating a Public Inspector of Charities, with an additional proviso that, when he was not actually employed in the inspection of almshouses, prisons and jails, in the State, he was to be the head of the Maryland Hospital for the Insane; and that, inasmuch he believed that there were certain members of the board who were hostile to him, it would be to his advantage to get rid of those people; and I was led to believe that I was one of the three selected. I don't know whether my name was mentioned or not.

By Dr. CONRAD:

Q. Did you not just now say that, prior to this conversation which you now repeat, which was held at Dr. Thom's house, you had not heard of this at all from me at the time you approached Dr. Thom, saying, that if you were not entirely satisfied in your mind in regard to the honorable intentions of Dr. Chancellor, your conduct would be different?

A. I said that it was my impression. I was not willing to state positively.

Q. You then had not heard from me, or from any one else, for ought I know, but at any rate you said that you had not heard that from me at that time?

A. Yes, sir.

Q. And you said that you had this conversation with Dr. Thom upon general subjects, and you remarked to him, that if you were perfectly satisfied in your own mind in regard to his honorable intentions, your conduct might be otherwise. You said just now that you did say that.

6

A. I don't exactly get your idea; state that again.

Q. You said, a while ago, that you said to Dr. Thom in a conversation held with him?

THE WITNESS:

That was not at his house.

Q. Prior to the one at his house, you said: " If I were entirely satisfied in my own mind in regard to the honorable intentions of Dr. Chancellor, my conduct might be different;" and I then asked you the question, what gave you that impression which that remark led you to make? What was the doubt in your own mind of his honorable intentions which led you to make that remark?

A. The doubt in my own mind was this: I did not exactly see what was the ground for such decided feelings upon so purely a trivial matter as an annual report to explain all the difficulty. I could not see the bottom facts of that thing, why, if there had been a difference of opinion merely in regard to a report, there should be such persistent hostility and such a row made about it. I could not have my mind made clear upon that subject. I was not present at the meeting of the Board of Managers, where this question of the two reports came up, and it was not until after that meeting adjourned that it came to my knowledge that there was a difference of opinion as to what should be done, and I never yet have been able to make my own mind perfectly clear as to why a difference of opinion on a question of that kind should have created such a difficulty. That was one thing, and if you will allow me to say it, another thing was this very thing I referred to in the first part of my testimony—in regard to this impression among some persons in regard to Dr. Chancellor's ambitions and prospects.

Q. Was that impression derived from any member of the board, either by implication or expression?

A. Not from Dr. Chancellor: not a single word was said.

BY THE CHAIRMAN:

Q. Did Mr. McCoy state that to you?

A. He told me about this other thing which occurred. I don't remember when.

BY DR. CONRAD:

Q. You just now stated to the committee that you did state to Dr. Thom that if you had been perfectly satisfied in your own mind of the honorable intentions of Dr. Chancellor, your conduct might have been otherwise. Now, I ask you the question, what was in your mind that produced a doubt as to what his intentions were? You answered that. If that doubt was not created by anything said to you by Mr. McCoy, or by any other member of the board, how did it arise in your mind?

A. It did not arise in my own mind, because Dr. Chancellor never said a word to me on the subject. Allow me to say, that those words, "honorable intentions," I have no recollection of making use of.

DR. CONRAD:

I think that is a matter of record.

THE WITNESS:

It is a matter of your own language. I was accepting the word "intention," but the word "honorable" was a word that I didn't say. Dr. Conrad originated the word three times.

THE CHAIRMAN:

And you adopted it?

THE WITNESS:

I did not take as much account of it as I should, but if I said it I should like to have it eliminated. I have no recollection of using that word, and I should like to have it replaced.

BY DR. CONRAD:

Q. What gave rise to that doubt in your mind? Was it anything derived from a conversation with any of the members of the committee or from any other source? Was it derived from Mr. McCoy's statement to you?

THE WITNESS:

Mr. Chairman, I would like to ask you a question. Would it be proper in me to state what occurred between members of the board and myself, in conversation?

THE CHAIRMAN:

Thoroughly so: each member of the board will come on the stand.

THE WITNESS:

To go back to the early history of the organization of this board: When the board was first organized, Mr. McCoy came to me and said, " Dr. Chancellor is certainly after something;" and I said, " What is your reason for thinking so? He said, " Dr. Chancellor came to me and dwelt largely upon his hospital experience, and upon his capacity, from the fact of that experience, to manage hospitals on an economic and satisfactory basis." I then, as I have stated, made the remark, as I have almost invariably made it, " no matter what his ambitions may be, the law absolutely precludes the enjoyment of that ambition, because he will have to serve without pay." I don't remember what his remark was in the conversation, but his expression was and my own feeling was, that Dr. Chancellor had an ambition. What it was, I never did know and never understood, until this statement occurred at Dr. Thom's house. Then, the way in which that was brought out was, in a conversation where we met Mr. McCoy on the street a day or two afterwards. Dr. Chancellor had been to me and had spoken of his large experience in hospitals, and how, from that consideration, he had been successful in managing them, and how it would gratify him to be appointed.

BY DR. CONRAD:

Q. You speak of this doubt arising in your mind in regard to Dr. Chancellor. What gave rise to that suggestion in your mind as touching this question just referred to, which was given to you by Mr. McCoy?

A. Nothing in the world but the conversation.

Q. There was nothing in your mind but the hospital?

A. We were speaking of the hospital. Of course the ambition referred to the Maryland Hospital for the Insane, but at the same time Dr. Chancellor emphatically and positively stated that there was no amount of money that could induce him to live on the place. I believe it has been, from the very first, appreciated and understood that Dr. Chancellor was in the board as the friend of Dr. Conrad. The impression exists in the board that Dr. Conrad went to Dr. Chancellor, and solicited to become a member of the board, with a view to being appointed superintendent. When the board was organized the chairman of the board appointed me as chairman of the committee on by-laws, and those by-laws we drew up in my office. We provided for the personnel of the establishment—that all who lived upon the property should hold office at the pleasure of the board. The Governor was present at part of that meeting when the by-laws were adopted. Immediately that the by-laws were adopted, I nominated Dr. Conrad for the superintendency. Dr. Chancellor seconded the nomination, if I mistake not, and, in addition to that, moved an increase of salary. I am not sure of that, but there was an addition made to the salary of fifteen hundred dollars, which was attached to the position of superintendent by law. In consideration of the laborious duties to be performed as superintendent, an addition of five hundred dollars was made to his salary for serving in this anomalous position of treasurer, while at the same time being superintendent. I am not sure whether this was done at the instance of Dr. Chancellor or not, but my impression is that it was.

Q. Now in regard to the ambition. I asked you the question, was that ambition which you say was created in your mind at the time of that conversation; I asked you then if that did not point in the direction of the hospital, and I think you said yes.

A. I thought that was the impression.

Q. Have you heard anything in regard to his desire to live in the city and visit the hospital on the general plan formerly adopted by Dr. Stenart, or any member of the board?

A. Yes, I believe I have.

By Dr. CHANCELLOR:

Q. Will you state who the member of the board was?

A. My impression is that that member of the board is Mr. McCoy.

BY THE CHAIRMAN:

Q. Give the substance of what the conversation was in regard to the non-residents and salary like Dr. Steuart's?

A. There was no mention made of salary like Dr. Steuart's. The impression made upon my mind was that he had this desire to be the superintendent of that institution with a salary attached—what salary I don't know—and to reside in the city. After this conversation I must confess that I, to a certain extent, agreed with him on that point. I could not evade the question. Then I looked in the proceedings of the legislature the other day and saw an account of a bill in the House of Delegates proposing the office of inspector of public charities, and a debate in the Senate upon a bill proposing to reorganize Spring Grove Hospital. and I was very much surprised.

Q. You thought that tallied with what you heard before?

A. That tallied with what Dr. Conrad told me; this reorganization of the board does not, however, in the slightest degree agree with the proposed organization.

BY MR. CONRAD:

Q. In the month of November, in Dr. Thom's house, did I not say to you there and to Dr. Thom, that Dr. Chancellor had said to me more than once during the past summer that he designed to have a bill passed by the next legislature creating the office of inspector of public charities of the State, and a section to provide that when not occupied in the specific duties of inspection, his whole time and attention should be given to the Maryland Hospital for the insane?

A. I don't recollect it being said more than once. I recollect you saying that he did tell you that; whether it was more than once I don't know.

Q. Did I not at that time also say that this bill was to cut down the number of members of the present organization for the purpose of getting rid of certain objectionable members of that board?

A. You did. I don't know that it was in November; I am not responsible for the month.

Q. It was prior to the meeting of the legislature?

A. Oh, yes: there is no doubt about that fact; it was prior to that time.

BY THE CHAIRMAN:

Q. Who did he tell you would have charge of that bill for the reorganization?

A. Mr. Gorman.

Q. And you say such a bill had been presented by Mr. Gorman afterwards?

A. I saw that the bill had been presented by Mr. Gorman. That does not correspond with the bill that was named to me.

Q. It was a bill for the reorganization of the hospital, was it not?

A. Yes, sir.

By Dr. PERKINS:

Q. How closely does it resemble that bill?

A. Not in any particular hardly. It reduces the number of the members of the board from Baltimore. I would like to say that the object of that bill is to distribute the interest over the State, and to make the people of the State, generally, more interested in the institution. My own idea is that the bill is calculated to distribute its membership over the State for the purpose of distributing the interest in the institution. I have reason to know that.

By Dr. CONRAD:

Q. Can you state on oath that that is the object of the bill?

A. I can state that that comes from a responsible person, and that information is derived from Mr. Gorman.

By Dr. THOM:

Q. You made reference to a conversation had at my house, during which Dr. Conrad had stated to you that Dr. Chancellor had proposed a certain line of conduct to be worked out in the legislature, the substance of which had just been gone over. Don't you remember that the occasion referred to by you, when you confessed to a great deal of feeling upon our meeting on the street, was subsequent to the evening, and in continuation of the subject-matter of the conversation referred to just now?

A. No, I don't.

Q. Did I not state, in jumping out of the carriage on the street, that I wanted to find your house and could not do so, in order to ask about the matter we were discussing? Do you remember that?

A. Yes.

Q. And you started, if I remember rightly, and commenced pretty much where we had left off a few evenings back—that this was a horrible thing that Dr. Conrad had told us of in regard to Dr. Chancellor's intention, which excited you, because it looked as if Dr. Chancellor intended by this legislative process to get rid of Dr. Brown—to cut his head off. In pursuance of the same object after this evening spent at my house, Dr. Brown stopped upon my getting out of the carriage, and we commenced the conversation on the sidewalk and talked over the matter a good long while. Is not that the case?

A. No, sir; I stated to Dr. Conrad that it was my impression that that conversation occurred prior to the meeting at Dr. Thom's house. I am now quite convinced, and it is not an impression, but it is a fact, that it occurred prior. The conversation that Dr. Thom refers to occurred on German street, very near the terminus of the car route, and I am almost positive that that conversation occurred then, because Dr. Thom met me on the street and said: " You are the very man i want to see "—something to that effect— and he said: " Where do you live?" or something of the kind. I was going on to finish my rounds, and he jumped in his carriage and I in mine, and we had it on both sides of the street, and talked it over pretty generally. I know that conversation occurred prior to this, because the day after that Dr. Conrad came to my office, and it was in connection with that visit to my office that I went to Dr. Thom to see if I could not reconcile differences, and it was upon the strength of that conversation that Dr. Conrad and I had a conversation. The German street conversation was a continuation of the other.

By THE CHAIRMAN:

Q. Did Dr. Thom stop you, or did you stop Dr. Thom, on the street?

A. I give that up.

By Mr. COMPTON:

Q. You stated that Mr. McCoy said that Dr. Chancellor had these ulterior purposes?

A. That was his impression.

Q. Did you give that as an impression, or state it as a fact?

A. I have just explained that. He said that he could not understand why Dr. Chancellor would come to him and take particular pains to lay stress upon his experience in the management of hospitals, unless he had an object in view.

Q. And he inferred that those were his objects?

A. Yes, sir. You said "purposes." I don't remember that there was more than one. In fact I don't remember that one from what he said.

Q. It was a suspicion of his?

A. A mere suspicion: nothing but a suspicion.

Q. You said that Dr. Conrad was an efficient and honest officer of the institution. Did you not vote to accept his resignation?

A. Most undoubtedly. I felt that Dr. Conrad had to withdraw. I am not satisfied in my own mind that a man is a first-class head of an institution who is as sensitive as Dr. Conrad is.

By Dr. CONRAD:

Q. When did you arrive at that opinion?

A. From the time I first knew you.

Q. Then why was I nominated by you?

A. Because I did not know you as well as I did after I was in the institution awhile. My acquaintance with you was merely nominal before that. When I speak of knowing him, I speak of contact with him in the institution.

Q. In what particular did that sensitiveness manifest itself? Was it in my official capacity towards you and the

board, or was I peculiarly sensitive about some aggressions
(as I considered)—I will hardly use that word, but some
things done by the board which were calculated to impair
my control of the hospital?

A. I don't really know that you have any right to com-
plain of any attempt on the part of the board to undermine
your authority. It was the common opinion of the board,
whenever a question was submitted to it, " What is the superintendent's view of this question." I don't believe there
has ever been an institution in this country where there was
greater deference paid to its head, except in one particular,
and that is where I disagree with the board, but it was merely
a minor difference—no offence. It was an invariable question in the board when a matter arose in regard to discipline,
" What is the superintendent's opinion about it." Therefore
it could not have been on the ground of any interference
with your authority. Dr. Conrad will remember, when
speaking about his sensitiveness, that he came to my office
once and said to me then, and on more than one occasion
when I have been at the hospital. " You haven't treated
me with proper respect." Said I. " I am not disposed to
hang upon my dignity at all, but I don't think that you have
treated me at the institution as you have others."

Q. Was that my sensitiveness or yours?

A. Chiefly yours. I was not discussing the sensitive
point, Your question was this, whether or not my idea of
your efficiency—

Q. I ask you that question, whether that was an evidence
of your sensitiveness or mine?

A. I will answer that as soon as I get through. The
question is whether that is an evidence of misconduct or
of sensitiveness, and I allege it as an evidence of misconduct. Upon the ground of his sensitiveness, I rarely made
a suggestion in the institution but what I feared I would
hurt Dr. Conrad's feelings.

By Dr. PERKINS:

Q. Is it not one of the peculiar traits of the profession
to be a little sensitive on all questions touching their peculiar rights?

A. You are as able to judge of that as I am.

BY THE CHAIRMAN:

Q. You say you were present when these reports were made up?

A. No, sir: I said I was absent from that meeting.

Q. You said you drew up the by-laws at your office?

A. The committee did.

Q. There the superintendent is made the head of the institution, and is required to report annually, as well as the president of the board, and to give his opinions upon all subjects relating to the hospital?

A. Yes, sir.

Q. Did you call the attention of the board, after you found out that they had suppressed a portion of it, to the fact that it was their duty to let it go in, no matter how it was?

A. My recollection upon that point is not sufficiently clear. My recollection is, that when the meeting took place which succeeded the one at Mr. Gunther's house, it was the opinion that whenever the report of the Board of Managers touched upon the management of Spring Grove Hospital for crazy people, to that extent it had exceeded its legitimate province, that all those questions belonged properly to the superintendent.

Q. And that the superintendent had the right to report side by side with the report of the Board of Managers?

A. I think the board had no feeling different from that. The board adopted unanimously the report of the superintendent that night with certain corrections. There were certain things left out, purely with reference to the propriety of having additional buildings put there, if I mistake not. We left that portion out and some other part.

Q. He said they needed none, and the Board of Managers desired some?

A. Yes, sir: they believed that it would be better to have some there.

BY DR. PERKINS:

Q. You state that there was at that time plenty of room

for patients and still unoccupied room there. Was the board acquainted with the fact that there was room there?

A. I didn't say that there was room there now: I said there was before.

Q. At the time this report was made was the board acquainted with this fact?

A. I am not able to say.

Q. Have you reason to think that they were?

A. I suppose so, because they inspected the hospital.

Q. And yet they suppressed that part of the report relating to that subject?

A. The report contained no reference to that subject. The report of the Board of Managers simply proposed to petition the legislature for sufficient money to increase the capacity of the institution, and Dr. Conrad's report. as I recollect, did not say anything about any empty room there.

Q. His report said that there was no necessity for that appropriation to make that addition?

A. No. sir. it was not upon that ground. The ground of objection was this: The Board of Managers all along have been left under the impression that if there was any one individual who was an advocate of the cottage system, it was Dr. Conrad. and when the board prepared its report through its president, advocating this increase in the establishment, you can imagine the surprise of that board when they found out for the first time that Dr. Conrad was not in favor of the cottage system as applied to those particular premises. for a reason which I believe to be good. I say this, that if we have difficulty in connection with water and sewerage there for a population of three hundred. we will certainly have greater difficulty if we have a population of seven hundred. But that had no reference to this vacant room. I believe.

BY MR. KNIGHT:

Q. Both the board and Dr. Conrad thought that more room was necessary to take care of the insane of the State. Dr. Conrad recommended buying a hospital in Frederick for that purpose, and the board recommended building cot-

tages upon the premises. · But they were agreed upon the
one point, that additional room was required?

A. Yes, there is no doubt about that.

BY THE CHAIRMAN:

Q. Provided they could get the paupers of the State gathered together?

A. Yes, sir. You understand that I was not at that meeting.

DR. CONRAD:

That point comes under the head in my report of " Further
Provision for the Insane"—looking to the future.

MR. COMPTON:

I desire to call attention to the eighth section of the law
in regard to the hospital, and to say in connection with that,
that my construction of Dr. Conrad's report and opposition
to it are based upon that section of the law. It was at the
time, and is so still.

Q. I want to ask your interpretation of the by-law considered in connection with that section.

The chairman decided that this is not a proper question
to be put to the witness.

Ex-Governor A. W. Bradford sworn and examined.

BY DR. CHANCELLOR:

Q. I wish only to ask you what relations, so far as you
are aware, had existed between Dr. Conrad and myself;
whether I ever canvassed you, as stated in one of the
charges, in reference to securing a position for myself?

A. I never heard nor witnessed anything leading me to
a conclusion anything like it. You have canvassed—and it
is the only canvassing I have ever witnessed from you in
connection with the subject—you have canvassed the board
with a good deal of assiduity, I think, and a good deal of
anxiety and solicitude, apparently; and after the organization of the board, and the election of the superintendent, I
remember that that canvass was simply to secure the consent
of the members of the board to go upon the bond of Dr.
Conrad. You stated to me, and, I think, you stated the

same thing to every individual member of the board, that
some difficulties were likely to arise in the power of Dr.
Conrad to give the required bond. You inquired of me,
on the subject, as to whether I would consent to go upon
the bond. I rather reprobated such a practice, and thought
it a bad precedent, and so expressed myself, but upon consideration, I agreed to it, and so did every member of the
board, I think. I never heard of any canvassing done by
you, except upon that single subject.

Q. I stated at the time that I myself was willing to go
upon the bond, and was the first to go upon it?

A. Yes; you expressed then, as you had at all times
done, the greatest concern and anxiety for the retention of
the presence of Dr. Conrad, and said that you went into
the board, as I understood, for the very purpose of making
him the superintendent: and all my observation tended to
confirm me that your chief object was to support him.

Hon. Henry D. Farnandis sworn and examined.

The witness stated that his sense of hearing was somewhat impaired, and therefore he preferred, if agreeable to
the committee, to make as full a statement upon the subject
under investigation as he could, and then to answer such in-
terrogatories as might be propounded. No objection was
made and the witness stated as follows:

When appointed a member of this board I received nu-
merous letters recommending different physicians for the
position of superintendent. The persons upon whom I
mostly relied, recommended Dr. Conrad. I came to Baltimore very much inclined to support him, and one of the
first persons I met was Dr. Chancellor, who promptly canvassed me and pressed upon me the claims of Dr. Conrad
as a physician of eminence, and a person of gentlemanly
character and peculiarly fitted for this position. In fact I
agreed to vote for Dr. Conrad, and did so. The next thing
I heard from Dr. Chancellor was that Dr. Conrad either had
some delicacy in applying to his friends, or some difficulty
in finding friends who would be his security, and I was

afraid he would have to decline the position on that account.
Dr. Chancellor said he should regret this very much. With
this understanding I, with the others, went on Dr. Conrad's
bond. and I have never seen any reason to regret it. I
thought Dr. Conrad fulfilled his duties admirably well.
I started with the most friendly feelings towards him, and
have never changed them, and so far as I know every
member of the board participated in that feeling. I know
that the largest liberty was given to Dr. Conrad, and the
largest discretion in choosing his employees; in fact in
everything he was consulted and generally yielded to. I
never saw any change in his feeling of any member of the
board towards Dr. Conrad until this matter of the report.
I was not present at the meeting when Dr. Conrad's report
was offered: I knew nothing of it, and went out to the hospital and there saw Dr. Conrad, who made some allusion to
the unpleasantness. but finding that I knew nothing about
it he himself told me his story, which I listened to carefully
and sadly. I was sorry that anything had occurred to trouble him or disturb the harmony of the board. After I had
heard his whole story I came to the conclusion that he had
put himself in a lamentably false position, and I frankly
said to him, "Doctor, you are wrong." He regretted that
I took that view of the matter, but I said: "I am satisfied
from your own version, which I assume to be correct, that
it must be the conclusion that every fair minded man would
come to, that you are wrong, and I think when the tempo-
rary passion subsides you will come to the same conclusion
yourself." I mention that, because as I have already said,
I was particularly gratified at the next meeting in seeing
produced by Mr. Compton, the chairman of the committee,
a letter from Dr. Conrad expressing his regret, and I did
not understand it as applying to this report particularly, but
it was a general apology for anything that he might have
done unintentionally or in passion.

DR. CONRAD:

Was not that letter an apologetic letter pertaining to two
questions? I stated to the committee, of which Mr. Comp-

ton was chairman, when my report was expunged, that the action of the board should go upon the minutes of the board. Great exception was taken to that statement. Mr. Compton stated at that time, "There is no objection." Dr. Chancellor, I understand, afterwards took violent objection to that remark. That was one of the remarks about which this letter was written. The other one was that I did state that the board should not have adopted the report of the president before the report of any of the departments of the hospital were made up. Dr. Chancellor took great exceptions to these two remarks. No other member of the board, I think—at least I have heard so—ever took offence. Mr. Compton is my authority, I think, for that statement. Was not that letter written in explanation and apology for those two things?

THE WITNESS:

I can only say that I am at a disadvantage, from not knowing exactly what the letter was in reply to. I only saw the letter. I was not present when the committee was appointed, and I didn't know the extent of their powers. I only saw the letter, and it was particularly gratifying to me, because, when there was some hesitation about it, I said: "Dr. Conrad, no doubt, did not mean to do anything wrong, and certainly that letter is wide enough to cover everything."

By Dr. CONRAD:

Q. Was not that letter satisfactory to every member of the board, and so expressed by every member?

A. As I understood, it was not only satisfactory, but it was formally received as satisfactory.

Q. Didn't Dr. Chancellor, subsequently, say that he was not satisfied with that letter?

A. No, sir. not subsequently: Dr. Chancellor said at the time that it did not cover everything. Somebody said that it was satisfactory, or something of that kind: I do not remember the words, and Dr. Chancellor said: "No, it does not explain some things" (the particulars of which I did not get) about Dr. Conrad's not giving him information about the names and pay of the employees, and then it was that I said: "I think that letter is wide enough to cover everything," and the question was put to the board, and the resolution was that it should be received as sufficient. I thought that ended the matter, and anticipated no further trouble. I knew of nothing further until I received the call to investigate the charges made by Dr. Conrad against Dr. Broome. I had a note from him telling me that it was important. When we met for that investigation the members of the board suggested that I should manage the examination of the witnesses. I supposed they did it for two purposes—it struck me so—because I had had some practice in examining witnesses, and they seemed to have regarded me as the peculiar champion of Dr. Conrad. I started into it with the determination that Dr. Conrad's charges should have a fair chance of being heard, and that he should establish them if he could. When we met, Dr. Conrad and Dr. Broome were called in, and Dr. Conrad asked that the witnesses be examined under oath. I said: "We have no right to administer an oath." He said he had a magistrate present for that purpose. I then explained to him that we had no right to require an oath, but that if it gave him or Dr. Broome any satisfaction, and if it added force to the solemn obligation on the part of the witnesses to tell the truth, of course any of the witnesses who pleased might be examined under oath. Dr. Conrad then said: "I may as well send the magistrate away." I said: "No, let him stay here, because you may wish to swear some of the witnesses." That was concurred in unanimously by the board; so that I am afraid the outrage there was mine. I did not see that we had the right to examine witnesses under oath, but I was willing, and every member of the board was willing, that any and every witness should be examined under oath who desired it. The examination was made very carefully, and the conclusion we arrived at was made known to Dr. Conrad and Dr. Broome. In a very few moments Dr. Conrad's note came in tendering his resignation. Before any action was had upon it another note came in

7

requesting an immediate interview with the board, which was promptly conceded. Dr. Conrad came in and said he had a request to make, which request consisted of three parts. The first was, that they would reconsider his resignation, and he wished that the board would reconsider the vote of censure upon him; next, that a committee should be appointed to investigate his accounts; third, that a committee should be appointed to investigate the state of the hospital.

Q. Will you state what was the occasion of that censure?

A. I will. I did not know that it was important, or I should have done it. The reason of the censure was this: That in the specifications (seventeen in number) which Dr. Conrad made, of course implying official misconduct in Dr. Broome, there was neither day nor date. When we came to fix the day and date, it turned out that none of them were particularly recent. They were simply matters of discourtesy, I think, and ran over a long period, of a year or eighteen months. One of the permanent rules of the institution in print is that it is the duty of the superintendent to report promptly any act of insubordination or misconduct on the part of his subordinates: and they thought that if Dr. Conrad, at the time of these offences, had regarded them of such importance as he seemed then to do, it was his imperative duty to have reported them, and in not doing so he had neglected his duty. I think that was the amount of the censure, and I think is expressed in the resolution itself. Dr. Conrad retired, and being still in the position of a friend of his, I said—"Gentlemen, I voted against that resolution of censure on Dr. Conrad. I did it because I am prepared to say that it is not right, and I did it because we are here to try Dr. Broome, and I do not care to try Dr. Conrad at the same time: hence I am technically against that resolution of censure, but if any gentleman here will move a reconsideration of the resolution, I will move to strike it out." There was a momentary pause, and then Dr. Brown moved a reconsideration, and I moved to strike it out, saying to the board they "might in-

flict some injury against Dr. Conrad, but by doing this you
will show him that you have no personal ill-feeling against
him," and I think it was stricken out.

By MR. COMPTON:

Q. Was not that done unanimously?

A. Unanimously: there was no objection at all.

Hon. Barnes Compton sworn and examined.

By DR. CHANCELLOR:

Q. I will ask you to make a statement in regard to my
official conduct in the hospital, and the relations which I
have sustained to Dr. Conrad from the time of the organization of the board up to the fourteenth of November, when
these reports were presented?

A. During the winter of 1876 or early spring: I cannot
fix the date.

MR. KNIGHT:

State what took place between that committee and Dr.
Conrad in regard to striking out certain portions of Dr.
Conrad's report.

A. I met Dr. Conrad here in Annapolis. I think it was
after the passage of the bill affecting the hospital by the
legislature of 1876. I met him upon the steps or at the
head of the steps leading up into the executive chamber.
He told me of his desire to obtain the position of superintendent of that institution. I expressed my readiness and
willingness to see him obtain that position. He requested
me, in connection with Dr. Chancellor and other friends, to
use what influence I might have to secure the appointment
by the Governor of competent men, of course, for the position of members of the board, who would not be hostile to
him. I promised that I would do so, and I did so. The
Governor made his appointments, and sometime, I think,
after the adjournment, sundry gentlemen, who were named
by the Governor for the position of managers, declined to
serve. Dr. Chancellor then came to me, being my family
physician and personal friend, and also the friend of Dr.
Conrad, and appealed to me to take a position on the board

as one of the managers, for two reasons, as I understood, one being that I might help his friend, Dr. Conrad. I said —" I won't ask for it, but, if the Governor puts me on the board, I will accept it and serve for your sake." I was appointed, and did accept the position, and have served since. When we elected Dr. Conrad superintendent and treasurer, sometime afterwards it was ascertained that he could not obtain the necessary bond, whereupon Dr. Chancellor appealed to me, as has been stated by other members of the board he did to them, to become Dr. Conrad's bondsman, that he might hold the position. I consented, and the whole board consented, and we went on his bond. From that hour up to the meeting of the board, when Dr. Conrad and Dr. Chancellor submitted their reports, whenever Dr. Conrad's name was mentioned by Dr. Chancellor to me, either in the board or out of it, it was in the kindest terms that one friend could use in reference to another, his object in every interview being, so far as I remember, to promote Dr. Conrad's comfort and interest in the institution. Previous to Mr. Gunther's appointment, I think Gov. Carroll appointed some one who declined, and Dr. Gunther's name was suggested to me, with the request that I would inform the Governor that he would make an admirable member of the board, and that he was a gentleman in every respect qualified, as well as a warm friend of his, and would be a friend of Dr. Conrad's. I so represented to the Governor, and he appointed Mr. Gunther, though other influences, of course, and other information were obtained by the Governor as to Mr. Gunther's character and standing, I presume. When Mr. McSherry, of Frederick, resigned, Dr. Chancellor himself approached me, and asked me to see the Governor, and recommend the appointment of Dr. Thom as a gentleman in all respects qualified, and a friend of his and Dr. Conrad's. I did so, and Governor Carroll appointed Dr. Thom, whether upon my recommendation or not I do not know. Those are instances which I remember particularly. I know that in the administration of the affairs of the hospital, whenever any trouble occurred, Dr. Conrad's friend in that board, and supporter upon all occasions, was Dr. Chancellor. I remember distinctly that when Dr. Conrad reported insubordination on the part of sundry employes of the hospital at a ball which occurred at Catonsville, he discharged them summarily, I believe, and requested confirmation of his action by the board. I remember that I, as one member of the board, was by no means prepared to second such summary dismissal. Mr. Davis, of Baltimore county, appeared there as the representative and friend of one of the parties who was discharged, and appealed to the board and protested against the discharge of that person. I think Dr. Chancellor in the board meeting was the first to speak and insist upon the endorsement by the board of Dr. Conrad's course, and state that we had no right to go behind his assertion to the board, and that, to maintain the discipline of the institution, Dr. Conrad must be sustained. I recollect that occasion distinctly. I recollect other occasions. I recollect the occasion when the matron of the hospital was discharged by Dr. Conrad.

DR. CONRAD:

She resigned: she was not discharged.

THE WITNESS:

I think however she resigned with your approval.

DR. CONRAD:

She did indeed.

THE WITNESS:

And that approval was indorsed by the board, although there were many members of the board who did not approve individually. But the act met with Dr. Conrad's approbation and the board thought it in the interest of the institution upon the whole, and for his well-being at the institution, that his course should be approved notwithstanding some of us did not approve of it. I think Dr. Chancellor was among the very formest to sustain Dr. Conrad's action.

BY DR. CONRAD:

Q. Do you know that I conferred with Dr. Chancellor and that it was only by his consent that those discharges were made? Do you also know that the place of engineer was supplied on the suggestion of Dr. Chancellor by the appointment of a friend of his?

A. I do not know that: I will tell you what I know. I know that any suggestion of Dr. Chancellor's to you, at one time, and from you to Dr. Chancellor, was tantamount to doing the thing itself—whatever it might be. I never saw two men with closer relations in my life.

DR. CHANCELLOR:

Don't you remember when some objection was made to Dr. Conrad's discharging these parties that I stated to the board that I had taken the responsibility to myself of approving the act of Dr. Conrad because I thought it was for the best interest of the institution?

A. I know you were prompt to indorse his action?

Q. And in regard to the engineer who was afterwards appointed, Dr. Conrad says a friend of mine, I never had seen him and did not know him. He was recommended to me as a competent engineer.

THE WITNESS:

I don't know that.

THE CHAIRMAN:

Go on.

THE WITNESS:

Generally, that is all I have to say. If you want me to go on and detail what came to my knowledge of after-troubles, I will do so. I will state, if desired, what I remember in connection with the elimination of portions of the report.

THE CHAIRMAN:

Go on with that.

THE WITNESS:

Before I begin that statement I want to ask Dr. Conrad, or any member of the board, if, in detailing my recollection in regard to matters as I shall attempt to do, my statement shall differ from their recollection, whether they will be kind enough to call my attention to the matters as I go along.

The board met to receive the report of the superintendent and president. The president of the board had been ordered by the board to prepare its report, having generally discussed what the condition of the institution was, what its needs were, and what was proper to be placed in the report. The board met, and the president read his report to the board, and it was accepted and approved. Dr. Conrad, the superintendent, then read his report. His report was a very lengthy one, and while he was reading it, as well as I remember, I turned to the law and read the section to which I have heretofore called the attention of the committee. Dr. Conrad's report went on to treat, at length, of a number of matters—almost everything in connection with the institution, its management, location, capacity, and what was the best in all regards, and dwelt at very great length upon the proper supply of water and the great trouble at the institution to get rid of its sewage. We had had on the premises an expert, Dr. Ames from Massachusetts, who had only a short time previous examined the locality and reported to the board a water shed competent to supply an almost limitless amount of water. He had also informed the board that it was perfectly practicable and feasible to dispose of its sewage. As I said, I turned at the time to the second section of the law and found that it required the board to report to the Governor generally in reference to the institution, and the superintendent being the treasurer, to report to the board specifically the financial condition, &c., of the institution. I will read that section which will illustrate fully upon what I grounded my first objection to Dr. Conrad's report.

"The Board of Managers shall annually, in the month of December, submit to the Governor a report showing the past year's operations and the actual state of the hospital and property in their charge; and, at the same time, transmit to the Governor the annual report of the superintendent and treasurer, which shall show all receipts and expenditures of every officer and employee, and the compensation of each."

My objection to the report was, that instead of simply doing that, it was occupying ground which properly belonged to the board to report upon.

By Dr. CONRAD:

Q. Do you remember in that connection the by-law, which, under the head of "Duties of the Superintendent and Treasurer," says: "At each annual meeting of the board he shall present a tabular view of the institution for the year, with full and minute details from the records, and accompanying it with a condensed report of other interesting and useful facts and circumstances, experiments and opinions, illustrating its management, condition and prospects." [Page 9, by-laws.]

A. I remember the by-law distinctly, and if read in connection with the section to which I have referred, I think it will show that your report exceeded even the large limit given in the by-law, and so thought at the time: and I made the specific point then which I make now, that your report does not comply with that section of the law, because you did not state the number of employees, or their pay, in your report.

Q. Was that ever called to my attention by the board?

A. I don't think you were present.

Q. Has it ever since been called to my attention?

A. No, sir; and I will show you why before I get through, I think. The board discussed the report, and without exception, as my recollection is, the board dissented from and objected to that large portion of Dr. Conrad's report which he read to the committee last night. However, the termination of the discussion was this: The report was referred to a committee of three, consisting of Governor Bradford, Mr. McCoy, and myself. It was late when we adjourned. I, as chairman of the committee, took charge of Dr. Conrad's report, the instructions of the committee being to report to the board at its next meeting what they deemed proper to do in the premises in reference to his report and the objectionable features in it. As I passed from the board-room to the door, on my way to the carriage, Dr. Conrad

met me and said: " Mr. Compton, will you be good enough
to allow me to have that report till Wednesday morning?"
(My recollection is, that we adjourned to meet at Mr. Gunther's house on Wednesday night.) I said, " Certainly you
can take the report, with pleasure, if you desire it," and I
handed him the report. On Wednesday, late in the afternoon, I returned to my house, not having received the report
up to that time. The hour was approaching for the meeting at the house of Mr. Gunther. I went to my room, got
pen, ink and paper, and sat down for the purpose of writing
out from memory what I deemed the objectionable features
in the report, and the reasons for the objections thereto,
designing to hand that to my colleagues on the committee
for their approval or otherwise, at our meeting that night.
I had not begun to write when Dr. Conrad's report, was
handed in at my door, and brought to me by the servant.
I opened it and found Dr. Conrad's report which he had
submitted to the board at the hospital, as I said last night,
minus the portion which he had in his possession here yesterday evening.

Q. Did not the committee, of which you were chairman,
exact of me the withdrawal of that portion of the report?

A. Never.

Q. They did not?

A. Never, sir: as a committee, never.

Q. Did not that committee, of which you were chairman,
and of which Mr. Gunther was a member, mark on that
paper such portions as were objectionable, and ask me to
read them and demand their withdrawal?

A. Never. I never saw you from the hour I handed you
that report at your request.

Q. At the meeting?

A. That was after the adjournment of the board, and I
never laid my eyes upon you or heard from you, directly or
indirectly, from the hour I handed that report to you, until
I received it at my house and reported it back to the board
that night.

Q. The board adjourned, but appointed a committee to wait upon me before they adjourned, did they not?

A. They did, and I have so stated.

Q. To see me and confer with me concerning this report?

A. No, sir: I never heard any such suggestion.

BY DR. BROWN:

Q. What was the office of that committee? What were they appointed to do?

A. I understood the office of that committee was, to take charge of that report, and knowing, from its intercourse with the board, what were the objectionable features of the report, and what were the views of the board with reference thereto, to make to the board, at its next meeting, a report of the judgment of the committee, as to how much of that report should be eliminated. That, I understood distinctly to be the design of that committee. But that that committee was authorized or directed to confer with Dr. Conrad, I never heard, and I state it distinctly, in the presence of my colleagues upon the committee. The committee never met, because the report was not in my possession. I hoped to get the report in time to call the committee together, but did not succeed in doing so. Now, last night, Dr. Conrad said that that portion of his report bore pencil marks, which pencil marks indicated the objectionable portions of the report. Those marks were never made by me nor Governor Bradford.

GOVERNOR BRADFORD:

I cannot say positively.

THE WITNESS:

If they were made by you. I call your attention to the fact that they were made not as a member of the board, but made by you during the time we were discussing it in the board. If Mr. McCoy made any marks upon that report he made them as Mr. McCoy—as an individual: but if he did it he did it without any conference with Governor Bradford or myself. Whatever passed between Dr. Conrad and Mr. McCoy, I never heard anything about, and the facts are as I have stated. In reference to what passed between Dr

Thom and myself, I would like to call Dr. Thom to the stand to corroborate what I say. I left my house after tea, with the report, in time to meet the board at Mr. Gunther's. When I left the Madison-avenue car I discovered Dr. Thom on the opposite side of the street, and I joined him. I said, "Doctor, I am delayed. I had taken off my coat and taken my seat to try to write from memory what I thought would be a proper report for the committee to make to-night, and just as I began the operation Dr. Conrad's report was handed in with all the objectionable features eliminated." Is that so, Dr. Thom?

DR. THOM:

That is so.

DR. CONRAD:

How could I have known what objectionable features were to be eliminated, and how could I have eliminated them so accurately as to suit your pleasure and purpose, without some knowledge from your committee to whom this report was referred?

THE WITNESS:

I infer from what you said last night that you saw Mr. McCoy. Did you see him or not?

DR. CONRAD:

Not to my recollection at present.

THE WITNESS:

Where did you meet that committee?

DR. CONRAD:

At the hospital. You were chairman of that committee, Governor Bradford was a member, and Mr. McCoy was a member. Governor Bradford handed me that report and said: "Here, Doctor, we want you to read this portion which is objectionable," and which had the two marks just as they are now.

THE WITNESS:

Now, I think I can give an explanation of that.

THE CHAIRMAN [Speaking of one of the pencil marks on the suppressed report]:

Did you ever see that mark?

A. I do not remember to have seen it.

Q. Did you ever see this other pencil mark?

A. I never did. I remember very distinctly that Governor Bradford, either in committee or in the board—my impression is, in the board—made some pencil marks on that paper while we were considering it.

Q. Was this mark on it when it was handed to Dr. Conrad?

A. I presume so. I never saw it. I never laid my eyes upon that paper. that I remember. since I handed it to Dr. Conrad.

GOVERNOR BRADFORD:

I cannot possibly recognize the pencil marks. but I do recollect making marks on the paper when it was read in committee as to the point of difference between that report and the report of the president. That was a board meeting instead of a committee meeting.

BY DR. CONRAD [To Governor Bradford]:

Did you not ask me to read it at the meeting of the committee?

GOVERNOR BRADFORD :

I did not make these marks anywhere except in a board meeting.

DR. CONRAD :

Did you not point me to that and say : " Doctor, here are these objectionable portions?"

GOVERNOR BRADFORD:

I think I did. I said. " How are these conflicting reports of yours and of the board to appear in the report of the committee?"

DR. CONRAD :

Was not Mr. Compton the chairman of the committee?

GOVERNOR BRADFORD :

He was: but it was not in a committee meeting; it was in a board meeting.

THE CHAIRMAN :

You made those marks?

GOVERNOR BRADFORD:

I cannot say so: I made some marks upon that paper of what I thought were not consistent.

THE CHAIRMAN [To the Witness]:

Did you see the marks?

A. No, sir: I cannot say that I ever saw them.

BY DR. PERKINS:

Q. This part eliminated at the suggestion of Gov. Bradford, and which is indicated by the marks, is the part that the committee, when considering it, considered objectionable, individually, if not as a committee?

A. No, sir; I said before, and I say again, that I have no recollection of any consideration of that part of the report by the committee.

Q. Is the part indicated by the Board of Directors, or the individual members of that board, the part to which the board objected as a board, or as individual members of the board?

A. The paper just now presented to me, I presume, is the same paper which Dr. Conrad had yesterday, and the part marked is the part of the report which, in the discussion of the report by the board, was objected to, as I understood, by all the board.

Q. If that part was not directly, positively, and officially condemned by the board, it was at least condemned tacitly and so understood?

A. It was objected to in words by the board, as I understood. My recollection is this: That Dr. Conrad, probably after discussion—of course it must have been after discussion by the board, and it may be after the committee was appointed—but when that discussion occurred, and while that board was in the hospital, my recollection is, that Dr. Conrad was in the room, and he was informed as to the objectionable features of his report.

DR. CONRAD:

You are mistaken about that.

THE WITNESS:

I may be mistaken, but that is my recollection.

DR. CONRAD:

I think I can refresh your mind on that. Do you remember that when you and Mr. Bradford and Mr. McCoy came

out with the committee, Dr. Chancellor came out at the same
time?

A. I will tell you why and how he came, if you will allow me.

BY THE CHAIRMAN:

Q. What was the committee appointed for?

A. I will tell you, as I have stated two or three times:—
That committee, composed of Mr. McCoy, Gov. Bradford
and myself, were appointed at that meeting to consider Dr.
Conrad's report.

Q. Did the board consider it either within their province,
or duty, or that they were warranted by law in suppressing
any portion of the superintendent's report?

A. Unquestionably I think it was within their province.

Q. And that is the reason, because you believed you were
warranted in law?

A. I did unquestionably, and I have just read the section
of the law which makes my mind perfectly clear on the
subject.

Q. I call your attention to the fifth section of the same
law:

"The Board of Managers may make, ordain, alter, amend,
or abolish all by-laws and regulations for the administration and government of said hospital, and the admission
and discharge of persons therein: which rules and regulations, in so far as they are within the power of said board,
and consistent with law, shall be binding on all persons
whomsoever."

Now I understand that your by-laws require this report,
and that it is consistent with the law for you to make that
by-law, and if so, how is a superintendent to do otherwise
than to make this report?

A. That is a question for the committee. I said in my
opinion he had not the right. [The chairman was about to
interrupt the witness with a question.] Please allow me to
finish my statement. I have this reason for wanting to finish it: A conflict of memory exists between Dr. Conrad and
myself, and I want to finish my statement on the subject.

I stated that I received that report at my house; that I took it to Mr. Gunther's house and submitted the report to the board with the objectionable features eliminated. That I met Dr. Thom on the street. During the session of the board at the hospital when Dr. Conrad's report was read, Dr. Chancellor, the president of the board, objected seriously to the report, and he evidently felt, and manifested that feeling, that his prerogative as president of the board had been encroached upon by Dr. Conrad. He manifested that feeling, and Dr. Conrad manifested some feeling. Dr. Chancellor took exception specially to Dr. Conrad's manner and some remark that Dr. Conrad made to the effect that he had encroached upon Dr. Chancellor's duties as president.

By Dr. CONRAD:

Q. Do you say that I said that?

A. I meant Dr. Chancellor. I say, too, that Dr. Conrad, when Dr. Chancellor manifested this feeling and submitted these criticisms, complained, as I understood, that Dr. Chancellor encroached upon his prerogative. He thought that Dr. Chancellor's duty was to submit the report to him and ascertain his views first. As I remember, he complained that he had not had time to make his report, and when Dr. Chancellor asked him if he had not agreed with him in certain matters, in which it seemed they differed, in his report, he said yes, but he had changed his mind. What I mean to say is this: That that and other things were said with some feeling by both Dr. Chancellor and Dr. Conrad. Afterwards Dr. Chancellor manifested the same sort of feeling. At that meeting at Dr. Gunther's it was thought that Dr. Conrad showed official discourtesy to the president of the board, and through him to the board, and the same committee who had had charge of Dr. Conrad's report (Governor Bradford, Mr. McCoy and myself) were appointed by the board to confer with Dr. Conrad, and ascertain what he had to say in reference to these matters. We went out to the hospital and saw Dr. Conrad, and there we discussed the report, and discussed what was desired in the board be-

tween Dr. Chancellor and Dr. Conrad, and, as I remember,
Dr. Conrad agreed to write a letter and did write one—if
I am wrong I hope to be corrected—and that letter was sub-
mitted, but not being satisfactory—

Q. Submitted to whom?

A. To the committee and the board, as I understood.

Q. Did you not tell me, in your office, about a week ago—

THE WITNESS [Interrupting]:

That is the first letter. He wrote two letters. A subsequent interview was had with Dr. Conrad by this committee
at the house of Gov. Bradford, where the whole matter of
these troubles was gone over again, and Dr. Conrad said he
would write and forward to the committee another letter,
and he did write and forward to the committee the letter to
which reference has been made here. That letter was read
and adopted by the committee, and its adoption recommended to the board, and the board accepted that letter as
entirely satisfactory, as has been stated here. That is my
recollection of the whole matter.

DR. CONRAD:

I was not before the board at any time.

THE WITNESS:

I did not say you were before the board. I said you were
present at the board when we were discussing it at the first
meeting.

DR. CONRAD:

I was not before the board.

THE WITNESS.

That is a question of memory with me, but that is my
recollection. That letter is upon the records of the hospital.

The committee took a recess to 5 o'clock P. M., at which
time the committee reassembled and Mr. Compton resumed
his testimony, as follows:

I should like to say a word or two in explanation of what
I said this morning—the committee will remember that a
difference of memory existed with reference to the occur-
rences which I have narrated, between Dr. Conrad and

myself, as to whether some things I said in reference to his report and the board occurred before the board or the committee. Dr. Conrad seemed clearly of the opinion, according to his memory, that this report was made by the committee. I thought otherwise, and that is my memory about the thing. Since then I have talked with Governor Bradford, who was on the committee, and he concurs with me in what I have said; and one other member of the committee concurs substantially with what I have said. I think Dr. Thom's memory of what occurred is somewhat different from mine. I only want to state again, as I said in the outset, that I was detailing the facts from memory alone and unaided except by conversations I have had with these gentlemen trying to refresh my memory, and, therefore, I was obliged to ask the members of the board to correct my memory, if possible.

BY THE CHAIRMAN:

Q. The board received the report from Dr. Conrad?

A. They did, and he read his report to the board.

Q. Have you ever had any report of his made before?

A. I think the Doctor reported in 1876.

Q. Was that report received then and published *in extenso*?

A. I declare I do not recollect now the circumstances attending the reception of the report at all. It is published in pamphlet form; I don't remember when that report was presented to the board at all.

Q. Was any committee appointed about it?

A. None that I remember.

Q. If his report had come up to the standard of the president of the Board of Managers, as to what they thought ought to be given in a report, would there have been any committee appointed?

A. I suppose not if the board had accepted his report.

Q. Then because of a divergence of the views between Dr. Conrad and the board, that committee was appointed, was it not?

A. That is my recollection.

Q. Now that committee was appointed with a view of

8

either having an elimination from that report, or else to get Dr. Conrad to modify it, if he did not do it of his own accord, was it not?

A. The report was referred to the committee, as I said this morning, according to my recollection and understanding, in order that the committee, being cognizant of the views of the board, might report to the board upon this report and eliminate from it such things as the board objected to.

Q. Do you mean to say that they were to eliminate without the concurrence of Dr. Conrad?

A. I do not remember that Dr. Conrad's concurrence was required.

Q. You don't know whether it was required or not?

A. I do not remember that it was.

Q. You stated this morning that it was a very great relief to you when you were about to start for the house where the meeting was to be held, that the report was handed to you with the objectionable features eliminated?

A. Yes, sir.

Q. You also said that you had sat down and prepared a paper?

A. No, I did not; I beg your pardon.

Q. You said then that you started to prepare a paper?

A. Yes, that I had taken my seat to prepare one.

Q. You had started to note down such things upon paper as you thought ought to be stricken from Dr. Conrad's report?

A. That is true.

Q. If he had not withdrawn these objectionable parts of his report, you would have reported to have them eliminated?

A. I should, as chairman, have prepared a report and submitted it to my colleagues on the committee; I cannot say whether they would have agreed with me or not.

Q. Then that would have been the report of your committee and not Dr. Conrad's report; it would have been his report as amended by the committee?

A. It would be such report as the board thought fit to accept.

Q. Did you conceive that the laws and by-laws warranted you in that?

A. I did.

Q. So that you were simply saved the trouble of striking it out before he had requested it, or before you had done it yourselves?

A. That is my recollection of it.

By SENATOR STUMP:

Q. Have you that second letter of Dr. Conrad's?

A. No sir; that letter is with the minutes.

Dr. Chancellor said that he had the letter.

Dr. Conrad said that he would like to have both the first and second letters read to the committee.

Dr. J. Pembroke Thom sworn and examined.

By DR. CHANCELLOR:

Q. I would like to have a general statement from you in regard to the matters of difficulty now under investigation, and also a statement so far as you know of the relations that existed between Dr. Conrad and myself.

DR. CONRAD:

Mr. Chairman, there was a great deal of that matter this morning brought before the committee which was evidence in no particular. I have not questioned the relations of friendship existing between Dr. Chancellor and myself; I am perfectly frank to admit them. There have been no charges that there was any difference between us in regard to our friendship, and the entire matter that was stated here this morning by Mr. Compton and by Mr. Farnandis in regard to that matter, and perhaps by myself, was entirely irrelevant, and was not evidence in any respect at all, and I consider that it is not proper. I am perfectly willing to admit all that has been said in regard to the friendly relations existing between Dr. Chancellor and myself, and in regard to any favors that he has ever shown me—I am perfectly willing to admit them all, but I do say that they are not evidence at all.

Dr. CHANCELLOR:

I simply state that if I mistake not there is a charge against me that I canvassed the board for the purpose of having myself elected superintendent; and if such were the fact when I was professing friendship for Dr. Conrad, surely I could not have been a faithful friend to him. I want to establish the fact that I never canvassed the board, and that my relations to Dr. Conrad were those of the utmost friendship from beginning to end.

Dr. CONRAD:

I acknowledge that; I acknowledge the relations of friendship.

THE CHAIRMAN:

I considered this morning, when that portion of the testimony which related to the procuring of the bond was given, that it was not at all relevant to the matters under investigation here. It would be a proper subject of inquiry to see whether or not Dr. Chancellor had canvassed any member of the board with a view of suspending Dr. Conrad, and I took no objection to that, as I wanted to give the widest range this morning. If you would confine yourself to the charge and leave out that matter about going on Dr. Conrad's bond, and procuring his bond, I think it would be preferable. [To the witness:] Proceed.

WITNESS:

I do not know that I understand the particular point upon which I am requested to make a statement. However, I will state that I entered the board, and I think attended the first meeting about the 19th of September, 1877. I found everything in a very agreeable condition, perfect harmony existing, as far as I knew and believe, on all hands. When the time approached for the board to make its annual report, the president, as I was told, had requested the superintendent to furnish his report as a condition precedent. Time passed on, perhaps two or three weeks—that is my recollection, and if I am wrong I hope to be corrected. The president, I think, at one of the meetings of the board, stated that the Governor was very anxious to get in the report of the board so as to enable him to make up his address to the legislature. The board then commenced the consideration of the different heads of their report, and after considerable discussion, arrangement, &c., the president was requested to draw up a report in accordance with the views expressed by the board, which he consented to do, it being understood, if not expressed, that this report should be submitted at the next meeting to have different parts eliminated, or to be accepted in part or in whole, and to be criticised, and the writer of it was not to feel wounded if any part or the whole was rejected. That was the idea.

BY THE CHAIRMAN:

Q. That was the report of the president and directors?

A. Yes, sir. The president consented to do that work, and did prepare a report; when it was finished (this is hearsay) he took it to the hospital and read it to his friends.

Q. You did not know that of your own knowledge?

A. I did not.

THE CHAIRMAN:

Dr. Chancellor will relate that.

WITNESS:

Then I will stop there upon that point. However, when the report came before the board, and was discussed in detail, certain parts were eliminated, interpolations made, &c. After it had been agreed upon, and the whole being in accord with what I had understood from Dr. Conrad were his views, with regard to this cottage system, he having originally suggested the idea to me, and given me a document upon that subject to read, which brought my mind to the conclusion that that was the best thing for that locality. After we had discussed our report, Dr. Conrad's report was read. I think you read it yourself: did you not, Doctor?

DR. CONRAD:

Yes.

WITNESS:

I was hardly ever more astonished in my life than when that report was read. The whole tenor and purport of it, so far as this cottage system and other matters were con-

cerned, was so diametrically in opposition to all I had heard
from the Doctor, previous to this time, that I could hardly
have been more astonished. I absolutely knew not what
conclusions to draw. After the Doctor left the room, the
board continued the discussion of the matter, and they were
all seemingly as much astounded as I was. Subsequently
thereto, a committee was appointed for the purpose of in-
terviewing Dr. Conrad in regard to the thing to find out,
according to my idea, what possible thing could have wrought
this change so suddenly in his mind, because our report had
been based upon what he stated were his views.

BY DR. CONRAD:

Q. Was that the construction of it?

A. I speak for myself: I was not a member of the committee.

BY THE CHAIRMAN:

Q. But you were there?

A. Yes, sir; I was present. If I had been a member of
the committee, I should have acted in accordance with the
idea I now state—that there must have been something or
other of an extraordinary character to have wrought such
a change so suddenly in a matter of so much gravity, and to
which he had given so much thought, that induced him to
write such articles as well as to speak. The committee discharged their duties. What passed there is merely hearsay.
I can only state that, in the meeting of the board, the report
of that committee was not satisfactory. Their report was
to the effect that Dr. Conrad had used language and man-
ners to this committee, which was representative of the
board, putting himself in opposition to the board and showing insubordination, bad temper, &c.

BY DR. CONRAD:

Q. Do you remember that language?

A. I was not at the committee, but the impression that
was made by the report of the committee on the board so
far as I, being a member of the board, was concerned—and
the members of the committee are here and they can speak
knowingly in regard to that—the impression was an exceed-

ingly disagreeable one, that Dr. Conrad, who has always been upheld by every solitary member of the board in his ideas of discipline, should now present himself as a noted instance of insubordination himself.

DR. CONRAD:

I would prefer that to come out in response to a question, as it is not matter of knowledge on your part.

A. I shall be glad to answer any questions that the chairman will put. I am giving a plain, unvarnished statement of the part I acted, myself, not officially at all. If I could ever lay aside official action touching matters connected with that institution, I meant to do so between myself and Dr. Conrad, in the fullness of my friendship for him, and for the president and every member of the board. The Doctor will please correct me if I make any wrong statements. After getting to the institution and going through a portion of it, or perhaps the whole, I told the Doctor that I had come out from purely disinterested kindness; that no human being knew I was coming, and no human being knew what I was going to say; and I said, "Doctor, there is a cloud no bigger than a man's hand that can be swept away so easily. There is not a man on that board, as far as I know, who does not entertain the kindest feeling toward you. Why not remove this cloud?" Then the Doctor expressed himself as gratified at my action in the premises, and I hoped that the whole thing would be gotten rid of.

Q. Was not my remark to you that I would sleep on your suggestion?

A. That you would sleep on my suggestion in regard to the removal of the cloud—was not that it?

DR. CONRAD:

Yes.

THE WITNESS:

I merely said that to show the kind of feeling and the different matters that entered into this seemingly great matter. Time wore on. There was a meeting held at Barnum's, prior to which, and I suppose actuated perhaps by the conversation I had held with him, the Doctor came to my house, accompanied by Dr. Brown: I do not know, either, that they came together.

DR. CONRAD:

We had agreed to meet there?

A. In pursuance of this very thing, as I understood. We discussed the matters there, and I endeavored in every possible way, arguing with Dr. Brown and Dr. Conrad, without saying a word to Dr. Conrad that he was in a state of insubordination—arguing the best I could, with the kindest feelings in the world, and merely desirous of bringing about peace and harmony in that institution. During that conversation a good deal was said, but having my mind fixed upon the one point (that which I have just stated), I paid but little attention until the Doctor said, in substance, this: " If I were in your situation I would feel and act as you do." Dr. Conrad said this to me, expressing his appreciation for my desire for reconciliation and harmony in the institution. He said, "If I were in your situation I would feel and act as you do, but you do not know Dr. Chancellor," or, words to that effect. Said I, " I have known Dr. Chancellor for a great many years." He said, " But you do not know" this, that, and the other. My mind being intent upon one point I did not care to discuss Dr. Chancellor. After a time Dr. Conrad said, in substance, that Dr. Chancellor proposed to bring about in this present legislature a different condition of affairs, and I think a bill was to be introduced for that purpose, or something of the sort, by which certain members of the board obnoxious to Dr. Chancellor should be retired. I know that Dr. Brown was to be one of those put out.

DR CONRAD:

I specified Dr. Brown and Mr. McCoy.

WITNESS:

My mind being intent upon this point, and not desiring to discuss Dr. Chancellor or anybody else, when he mentioned that, Dr. Brown sprang up and said: " That is the worst thing yet." That called my attention to it.

By Dr. CONRAD:

Allow me to correct you there. My remembrance of Dr. Brown's remark is, "Is it possible?" Do I call it to your mind?

THE WITNESS:

No, my recollection is what I have stated—"that it is the worst thing yet," because Dr. Brown had been listening more closely to what he had said against Dr. Chancellor. It did not impress me as it seemed to impress Dr. Brown. We discussed the matter until about three o'clock in the morning. This committee in the meanwhile had been in the discharge of its duties, but I think it was that night that Dr. Conrad left with me a letter which I found on my table for me to convey to the board, which might be designated as letter number one. I do not know whether that letter is here or where it is. I have not read it for a long time.

Senator Stump moved to have the letters read before the committee, they being present in the hands of Dr. Chancellor. The chairman decided that they could not be read at this time, but should be produced and read by Dr. Chancellor when he should come upon the stand. From the decision of the chair Senator Stump appealed to the committee. The chairman submitted the question of appeal to the committee, and the decision of the chair was sustained by a vote five ayes to four noes, as follows: *ayes*, Messrs. Bannon, Cooper, Acton, Sander and Perkins: *noes*, Messrs. Stump, Knight, Brown and Houston.

THE WITNESS:

The letter which was left at my house by Dr. Conrad which I designated as number one, and which I took to the board as in duty bound, was of a similar—

SENATOR STUMP:

Do not state as to its character, if you please.

THE WITNESS:

Then letter number one was not satisfactory to the board. A committee was appointed for reasons which that letter

would indicate to put before Dr. Conrad the reason why
that letter was not satisfactory to the board. That committee subsequently interviewed Dr. Conrad. and met. as I was
told. in the city. where the Doctor was perhaps present at
Govenor Bradford's house. That elicited letter number two.

THE CHAIRMAN:

If you were not at the committee do not state.

WITNESS:

I was not. I was at the appointment of the committee.
The result of the appointment of that committee, and its
work. was letter number two. The committee in reporting
embodied that letter as a portion of their report to be spread
upon the minutes. That letter is in existence. and will appear at the proper time as just decided. In the meanwhile
I went to the asylum again, perhaps prior to this letter number two. and saw Dr. Conrad again. The place of this
meeting. when the committee was appointed, was at Barnum's; I should have stated, Dr. Conrad stated, "Doctor, I
was in the city when you gentlemen were in session at Barnum's. and as I rode out of the city for the first time it
came over me what you were after in your talk with me."
Said he. "Doctor, my impulse was to go in the first place
and write a letter down to the board telling them that I was
wrong." Well, now. said I, "Doctor, there is the whole
thing." Said I, "I did not like to tell you you were in a
state of insubordination."

DR. CONRAD:

There is the letter. which will speak for itself.

WITNESS:

Said he. "I must have been in a state of insubordination,
and I now recognize—

DR. CONRAD:

Did I state that I was in a state of insubordination.

WITNESS:

You did: that is my clear recollection.

DR. CONRAD:

I did not use the word "insubordination" at all.

WITNESS:

My impression is that you did. I did not like to use it. Said I, "Now you recognize the fact that you are in this condition, but I did not like to tell you, a gentleman like myself, that you were insubordinate;" but, said I, "If you will remember all that I have said, it pointed in that direction." Said he, "Doctor, now I am wrong." Said I, "That is all; we are getting right now." Said he, "What are we to do?"

Q. Where was that conversation?

A. It was in the board-room of the asylum.

BY THE CHAIRMAN:

Q. What time was that, in what year?

A. I think it was in the month of November, 1877. Said he, "Well, Doctor, what shall I do?" Said I, "I cannot put words in your mouth any more than I can put feeling in your heart. My impulse is, and my effort is, if I feel that I have done wrong to any man to go and tell him so," but I said, "You must pursue your own course." The result of that will be found doubtless hereafter. I do not know that I have any further matters to relate in connection with this. If there is any gentleman can suggest anything, I shall be glad to state what I know.

SENATOR STUMP:

I cannot ask you any question until these letters are read.

BY MR. KNIGHT:

Q. When did you enter upon these duties?

A. The 19th of September.

Q. The report was made the same year?

A. Yes, sir.

Q. The report of president and directors of the board was based, to a certain extent, I suppose, upon the opinions expressed by Dr. Conrad, as to the proper way of conducting the hospital, &c.?

A. Certainly; so far as that portion of the report is concerned, it was based upon what Dr. Conrad had observed.

Q. Between September of that year and November?

A. Precisely.

BY THE CHAIRMAN:

Up to the making of that report he was on good terms with the board, was he not?

A. He could not possibly have been upon better terms, so far as I knew.

Q. And the divergence of friendship and views had sprung from that written report of his?

A. From that period; yes, sir.

Q. Beginning when he handed in his report?

A. So far as I know. I was not aware of the true inwardness of anybody, but it seemed to me that it was all fair, friendly and harmonious in every view before that.

Q. And the offence there was because his report was not in unison with the report of the president and directors, was it not?

A. I do not know whether I can accept the word "offence."

Q. If not, I will qualify it?

A. That seemed to be the beginning of all the woes.

Q. When he handed in that report and a committee was appointed to get him to withdraw the objectionable part of it, that was the beginning of the trouble?

A. I do not know that I can accept that.

Q. What do you accept?

A. I was not on the committee, and I can only give impressions with regard to the duties of the committee.

Q. Were you present when that committee was appointed?

A. I was.

Q. Then if it was not for that purpose, what was it appointed for?

A. As I stated a little while back, I think it was to get at the fact as to how Dr. Conrad could in so short a time have come to a conclusion so diametrically opposite to that which he had previously held: one of the things was to investigate that.

Q. But suppose you had found out that he had changed his opinion in a day and had frankly said so, and the report back was that he had changed his opinion, say last night, then was that simply the duty that the committee was ap-

pointed to perform, or was it to get him to change his
opinion that he had written and to give another written
opinion, so as to cover your report?

A. I cannot answer the question, because I do not know
the verbiage of the resolution appointing the committee: I
can only give impressions.

Q. Have you got that resolution here?

A. No, sir; I have not.

BY DR. PERKINS:

Q. Are the proceedings of your board here?

A. Yes, sir: I question very much whether anybody can
read them though.

BY THE CHAIRMAN:

Q. Have you ever been connected with an institution of
this kind having several departments in it before?

A. No, sir.

Q. You have a superintendent's department in this institution?

A. There is a superintendent's department.

Q. You have a steward's department, entirely separate,
have you?

A. Yes, sir.

Q. Have you still another, the matron's department?

A. I cannot answer your question with the precision I
would like, but can only give impressions. There was a
lady in that institution at one time called a matron, and I
presume that her duties were those of matron.

Q. How many people had to make a report to your board;
how many departments?

A. All the reports of the departments, as I understand,
center in one person, to wit: the superintendent.

DR. CONRAD:

The report shows all; there are five reports.

THE WITNESS:

Then five reports come to the superintendent, and the superintendent reports to the board.

BY THE CHAIRMAN:

Q. Do you tell me and this committee that you made up

the president's and directors' report without getting any of these reports in upon which you have to base your report?

A. We did not have the *lex scripta* I suppose, but we had facts. The gentlemen of the board were in constant association with the superintendent, and with all the different officers of the institution. It is not necessary for matter of information except matters of statistics and figures, that they should be able to give a general report in regard to these matters.

Q. You mean to say that you could give a general report of the treasury department without the report of the treasurer, do you?

A. No, sir: I do not mean to say that that could be done at all.

By Dr. CONRAD:

Q. At the time of the writing of the president's report to the board and subsequently, had there been any report from the superintendent, treasurer, steward, matron, or farmer, before the board?

A. Not to my knowledge.

By Mr. KNIGHT:

Q. You received quarterly reports, did you not? Were they submitted to the superintendent?

A. I cannot recollect. I have been in the institution only a short time, since the 19th of September if I remember rightly, on to some week in November, and this was my first experience, so that my experience in this matter was very limited in regard to the manner of making up reports. It was an inference of mine that these things would all come through the superintendent, and that he would pass them over; I have had no direct experience.

By The CHAIRMAN:

Q. The question is simply a categorical one, whether or not these other reports were before your board before the report of the board was made?

A. There were reports, to my knowledge, before the board. The finance committee, perhaps, has a report with regard to the finances, but I am not on that committee.

The executive committee was in the habit of making reports, as was the finance committee, and the purchasing committee was in the habit of making reports to the board as they went along.

Q. The president and directors' report was founded upon nothing but the absence of all the reports of the other committees. They were founded upon conclusions without ever seeing any of these other reports. Do I understand that?

A. No, sir; you understand me that so far as figures were concerned, those things were gotten from Dr. Conrad's report, I think.

Q. He says he had only finished his report that day.

A. And our report was discussed, you understand, and not completed up to a certain time. We had Dr. Conrad's report in, and a great many matters were discussed, of a character which were pertinent to our report, such as figures, &c.

Q. But you say that the difference sprung up between you was because the superintendent's report did not tally with the report of the president and directors, which had already been in?

A. Not in regard to the question of figures, but in regard to the cottage system.

Q. Now about the opinions, judgments and conclusions, for you have stated that the divergence sprang up because Dr. Conrad had expressed a different view from the president and directors?

A. That portion of his report was astounding, and not at all to the taste or ideas of the board.

Q. Do you know that it was right that that report should go in, whether it agreed with their taste or not? Did you know it was right that that should go in without the crossing of a "t" or the dotting of an "i," just as he made it, so as to enable the legislature to have the different views of the officers of the institution?

A. I did not.

Q. Do you call that his insubordination, or was it because

he would not conform his opinions to those of the board that you hold him in insubordination?

A. Not at all.

Q. What was it?

A. His manner to the committee representing the board, as reported by the committee on the occasion of this visit to the hospital.

Q. You say that letter number one, mentioned here, was written at your house?

A. Not letter number one.

Q. What did you say about that?

A. I say that letter number one was left at my house by Dr. Conrad, and that I took it to the meeting of the board.

Q. At what time was that?

A. I stated that it was between September and November, in the month of November I think; that is my impression.

Q. You further stated that while he was there the committee were somewhere else?

WITNESS:

While he was where?

THE CHAIRMAN:

While he was at your house.

A. No, sir, not at all.

Q. What do you say now?

A. I say that Dr. Brown and Dr. Conrad were at my house to a pretty late hour, and brought letter number one, which, when the board met at Barnum's, I took there, and it proved to be not satisfactory to the board.

Q. The whole board were there or the committee?

A. The board, not the committee.

Q. What time was that?

A. I cannot recall dates. I am very bad at dates. You could perhaps recall, Doctor, when that meeting was at Barnum's that I refer to. I cannot tell you the exact date. There were a number of meetings growing out of the condition of affairs.

Q. Was it before this legislature assembled?

A. I could not answer.

DR. CONRAD:

It was early in December, I think.

THE WITNESS:

I would rather take the Doctor's recollection than my own.

BY THE CHAIRMAN:

Q. If the mere fact of his writing the report which was objectionable to the board of trustees or managers was not the act of insubordination alluded to, will you be kind enough to explain what was the act?

A. It was his language and bearing to the committee, as represented to the board by the committee, which was the creature of the board.

Q. It was not to the board?

A. It was to the committee, and reported by the committee to the board.

Q. You do not know it?

A. I was not there.

BY SENATOR STUMP:

Q. Had Dr. Conrad at that time made up his pay-rolls and his reports as treasurer and superintendent?

WITNESS:

At what time?

SENATOR STUMP:

At the time of this meeting.

A. There have been so many meetings referred to I scarcely know which you mean.

SENATOR STUMP:

I mean in November, at the time the board met for the purpose of making up this report to the legislature. At that time had he made up his report of receipts and expenditures of money, and furnished it to the board?

A. I could not answer that positively. I have the impression that there were data there.

Q. In his report?

A. The data were in his report, if my memory serves

9

me, but there were data I think on the table at the time
when these different propositions were being discussed.

Q. Were those data furnished by Dr. Conrad at that
time?

A. I presume the information had been furnished from
some source.

Q. Did the matron report directly to the board, or to the
superintendent?

A. The matron should always report to the superintendent. and I presume did; that would be the regular line of
discipline.

Q. To whom did the steward report?

A. I presume to the superintendent.

Q. Then the superintendent's report would be based upon
the reports of the matron, the steward, and the farmer?
Was that data furnished you at that time?

A. I cannot answer positively.

Q. Was anything eliminated from Dr. Conrad's report
which is required under the section of the law creating your
board?

A. There was nothing eliminated to my knowledge by
the board.

Q. You have by-laws?

A. Yes, sir.

Q. And those by-laws are for the regulation and control
of that institution among yourselves?

A. Yes, sir.

Q. They have the force of law among you?

A. Yes, sir.

On motion of Mr. Knight, the committee adjourned to 9
o'clock A. M. to-morrow, March 22, 1878.

MARCH 22, 1878.

The committee met pursuant to adjournment; Senator Bannon in the chair.

Present, a quorum.

Francis White affirmed and examined.

BY THE CHAIRMAN:

Q. Are you a director and manager of the Spring Grove Hospital?

A. I am.

Q. Are you aware of this trouble between Dr. Conrad and Dr. Chancellor?

A. About as much aware of it as you have heard stated here; the general features of it as far as it came under the cognizance of the board?

Q. Have you any statement to make?

A. No, not particularly.

BY DR. CHANCELLOR:

Q. I wish to ask Mr. White whether, at any time since our connection with the institution, he has had any cause to believe that I desired, or was taking any steps to secure, the position of superintendent of the hospital?

A. I never did think so.

Q. And I would ask whether in my conversations with you, in reference to Dr. Conrad, you did not think that I was really a friend of his?

A. I always supposed so.

Charles G. Kerr sworn and examined.

BY DR. CHANCELLOR:

Q. Did I not approach you in April or May, 1876, and ask you if you would consent to go upon the Board of Managers in the place of one who had declined an appointment, and did I not state to you specially that I desired you should go upon the board as a friend of, to the appointment of Dr. Conrad as superintendent?

A. I will state in reply to that question, that I cannot remember the precise month, but it was somewhere about that time. Dr. Chancellor came to me and told me that there was a vacancy on the Board of Managers of this institution, occasioned by the refusal of some gentleman to accept an appointment, and told me substantially, as Dr. Chancellor has stated, that he was extremely anxious to have Dr. Conrad made superintendent, and that he desired to get on the board gentlemen whom he knew would be favorable to Dr. Conrad's appointment; and he asked me if I would take the position, referring to the fact that he had heard me speak in very high terms of my knowledge of Dr. Conrad's efficient and intelligent management of the Marine Hospital during the time I was a member of the city council. I declined the offer, and that was the whole conversation.

Hon. Barnes Compton recalled.

THE WITNESS:

Mr. Chairman: I ask to make a statement in justice to myself, in reference to my testimony. It is this: When I testified here the other day, as I told the committee, I was testifying entirely upon memory and without any data or facts with which to refresh my memory. I gave what was my distinct recollection of all the facts; Dr. Conrad differed with me; and, as I said to the committee yesterday, I talked with Gov. Bradford and he agreed with my recollection of the facts. I had some slight talk with Dr. Thom, who differed from my recollection of the facts. Since then I have seen these letters, and the written letter calls to my mind the fact, that I was mistaken in one statement which I made, namely: That what I read as occurring between Drs. Chancellor and Conrad, occurred at the board meeting. A statement in the letter confirms me in the opinion, now, that I was mistaken. That conversation occurred at the committee meeting, and the reason why I confounded the two was the fact that Dr. Chancellor accompanied the committee to the hospital. All the other facts that I related I repeat.

BY DR. CONRAD:

Q. That was one of the points I wished to refresh your

memory upon, but it is now unnecessary. But there are some other questions I desire to ask you. You acknowledge then, that that was at a committee meeting of which you were chairman?

A. Yes, sir. And I will state in that connection that Gov. Bradford, acting as chairman of the committee, held the paper; I did not touch it.

Q. You remember that I stated, when Gov. Bradford handed me this paper, which was marked at that time, and asked me to read those marked sections.

A. No, indeed, I do not. I remember that the whole thing was gone over.

Q. You remember that I read a section which was presented to me by that committee?

A. My recollection is that the whole report was gone over. I think you read the whole report, and my recollection is that the whole thing was discussed, more particularly the objectionable portion.

Q. At any rate, you remember that I asked there, after this portion was rejected by the committee, that it should go upon the minutes of the board?

A. I remember this.

Q. Do you remember that?

A. I remember that you asked that the report be spread upon the minutes of the board.

Q. And you replied that you had no objection?

A. I do remember that, and I will state all that occurred if you desire.

Q. Do you remember that in answer to a question put to me by Dr. Chancellor, who was present at that committee-meeting, I remarked, that the error committed by the board in reading and adopting its report before any of the reports of the different departments of the hospital were in, was what had produced the collision?

A. I remember that you remarked, with a good deal of feeling, that it was highly improper in the board.

Q. I believe that is the word that is ascribed to me?

A. That is my recollection of your remark—that it was

highly improper in the board to make a report without first
receiving your report.

Q. At that time was the first remark (namely, the spread-
ing of the rejected report on the minutes of the board)
offensive to you, personally?

A. It could not have been, because I said I had no objection.

Q. Was the second remark objectionable to you at the
time?

THE WITNESS:

To me, personally?

DR. CONRAD:

Yes.

A. No, sir.

Q. Was the report of this committee to the board that
those two remarks were objectionable?

A. It was the character and manner of the remarks which
was objectionable and offensive to Dr. Chancellor and the
committee, and the board thought they had good ground
for taking exception and offence to such remark.

Q. That is not an answer to the question. I ask if the
committee made that report to the board in respect to these
two remarks made by me: or did the committee subsequently adopt that opinion after hearing the statement of
Dr. Chancellor's personal views about the remarks?

A. I think that opinion was entertained by the committee
at the time the remarks were made.

Q. You just remarked that you, as chairman, did not?

A. They were not offensive to me, but to Dr. Chancellor.

Q. You were chairman of the committee?

A. Dr. Chancellor was *ex officio* a member of the committee and was present.

Q. He was *ex officio* a member of that special committee?

A. You are right about that: it was a special committee.
You asked me something about the report of the committee
to the board: what was it?

Q. I asked you if the report of the committee to the
board was that those two remarks were objectionable, or

was it the impression produced on the committee subsequently by Dr. Chancellor's objection to the remark?

A. My recollection is that the committee reported nothing to the board except the fact that I had received from you, for the committee, a report with the objectionable parts eliminated.

Q. Did you not say that, "If that report goes before the legislature we will receive no appropriation?"

A. I said that I did say so, and I repeat that, and, as I think, for good and sufficient reasons.

Q. Now why should the report of a superintendent be more potent to prevent the result desired by the board, than the report of the board itself?

A. I do not say it would be; and I do not think it would be.

Q. You stated that if that report came before the Legislature the board would receive no appropriation; you acknowledge that?

A. I repeat that now.

Q. Then that statement must have been based upon some fact in your mind. Now why should the report of the superintendent be more potent to prevent that result than the report of the board itself? Was it not because the arguments contained in the superintendent's report to the contrary, were more in accordance with the facts?

A. Not a bit of it, in my humble opinion.

Q. You are the treasurer?

A. You know that fact.

Q. You are the manager of the Maryland Hospital for the Insane?

A. You know that fact, too.

Q. Now I wish to ask you, was it more consistent with your duty, as a member of the Board of Managers, to suppress a report of a superintending officer for the purpose of obtaining an appropriation from the State, for the institution of which you are a manager, than it was with your duty as treasurer of the hospital?

A. I am not on trial, but I will answer that question.

Q. You are the witness.

A. Yes, and I will answer these questions. I do not see their pertinency, or bearing, or meaning, but I will answer them.

Q. You " Do not see the meaning?" I will take you up at that point.

A. I will answer your questions one at a time.

Q. How can you answer questions if you do not see the meaning?

A. I will answer your questions one at a time, and in my own way, and no other way. I objected to that portion of your report which was eliminated, and I said in that connection, that if that report was presented to the legislature, it was my opinion that the legislature would make no appropriation. I say again that if that report had been presented to the legislature, and the legislature had received information therefrom, and believed that there was any foundation in fact for the report, or that such things existed, it would not have been proper for the Legislature to make an appropriation. I say again, that my reason for desiring to see that portion of that report eliminated, was simply that I did not believe it was in accordance with the facts relating to the hospital. I think that your statement in regard to the insufficient water supply was not a fact. I believed that your theory, that the sewerage could not be disposed of, was incorrect; and that your theory in regard to having cottages upon the ground was entirely erroneous. And your report being made to that effect, and contrary to the report of the board, would have raised a conflict between the superintendent and the board, and would have confused the minds of the members of the legislature, and have raised a question of veracity.

Q. You stated that you could not agree with the facts as stated in regard to the sewerage and deficient water supply. Have you ever examined the water supply carefully, and have you ever measured the amount of water discharged in the dry season? In short, had you any basis of fact to go upon, from your own examination, in wanting that fact eliminated from the report?

A. No, sir.

Q. Then how can you form such an opinion?

A. Because I was upon the ground with a gentleman noted as an expert in such matters, who, after a careful examination of the ground, reported to you, or said in your presence, that there existed a water shed which would supply an almost limitless amount of water.

Q. If you were a commissioner to build a hospital of the capacity of five or seven hundred patients, would you, even upon the report of that sanitary engineer that there was an underlying water shed, from fifteen to forty feet—the depth unknown— would you, upon that ground, put the building at that place?

A. I say this: that that statement being made by Dr. Ames as in contradiction to a statement made by Dr. Conrad, I would unquestionably base my opinion upon Dr. Ames's statement.

Q. If you were a commissioner to place property of the State, to the amount of ninety thousand dollars, upon a piece of land, where, up to that time, there had been a fear of deficiency of water, would you, upon the mere statement of an engineer, of whom you knew nothing whatever except from reputation, and that reputation limited—would you locate the property of the State at that point, knowing that the essential element of water would be an important factor in the ultimate management of the institution?

A. Knowing that the essential element of water would be an important factor—an absolutely necessary factor with any institution in which there are three, four or five hundred human beings to be accommodated—I would not hesitate for a second, if a man whom I believed to be a competent engineer thought that a sufficient supply of water could be obtained.

Q. And you make the same statement in regard to the sewerage?

A. I do. We have to depend in these matters upon the opinions of experts who are informed on such subjects.

BY MR. KNIGHT:

Q. Did you ever have any conversation with Dr. Conrad himself, in regard to the location of the cottages?

A. I think I have incidentally heard him discussing that matter with other members of the board. I do not remember ever to have had any conversation with the Doctor myself.

Dr. C. W. Chancellor sworn and examined.

BY THE CHAIRMAN:

Q. You may make whatever statement you desire in your own way, and then any questions may be put to you that the gentlemen may desire.

First Charge Read.

THE WITNESS:

Mr. Chairman, I think that charge has been already sufficiently answered by each of the members of the board, who have heretofore testified that I never canvassed them for any appointment as the chief officer of the board. I will state, however, that in March or April, 1876 (I think it was during the session of the legislature), a gentleman came to my house, who was unknown to me, and presented a letter of introduction. He stated that he came to see me with reference to a contemplated reorganization of the Spring Grove Asylum, and stated that some friends of the institution had requested him to see me, and ask whether I would consent to accept the position, which Dr. Steuart then held, of president and superintendent of the institution. I stated to him that I would not do so under any circumstances; that I would not occupy the position for ten thousand dollars a year; and furthermore, that I had consented, at the request of Dr. Conrad, as his friend, to go on the Board of Managers with a view of electing him as superintendent, and that I would not, under any circumstances or for any amount of money, violate my plighted faith to Dr. Conrad; that he was a personal friend of mine, and I earnestly desired to see him put in that position. My actions since I have been in the board, and the manifestations of friendship which I have always shown to Dr. Conrad, have been abundantly testified to by the witnesses who have preceded me, and I, therefore, will not take up the time of the committee for anything further in regard to that.

By Dr. CONRAD:

Q. I desire to ask if you have not, once and more than once, said to me that you intended to have a bill passed by the next legislature creating the office of inspector of public charities, and that a section thereof would specify that said officer should, when not employed in his duties, visiting and inspecting almshouses, jails and prisons, give his whole time and attention to the Maryland Hospital for the Insane? And did you not ask me for the report of Dr. Langmicy, stating that this would not affect my position and my relations there; that I would remain there just as I was?

A. The details I do not remember, but I will state what transpired.

Q. And let me say further—

A. Let me make my statement first, if you please. I had a conversation with Dr. Conrad, which was substantially as stated, and that I made public. There was no intention on my part to conceal anything in regard to that matter, and I published in this report what my views were. It was during the time that Dr. Conrad and myself were making our visitation to the almshouse. We talked over the subject of the condition of the almshouses and agreed that the best plan would be to have an inspector of public charities, whose duty it should be to visit these almshouses and give such instructions as, in his judgment, he might see fit. I will ask the clerk to please read those two portions of my report, which will show what my views were and the views which I stated to Dr. Conrad.

The clerk, as requested, read the following from page 25

of the report on public charities, reformatories, prisons, and almshouses of the State of Maryland, made to Governor Carroll, July, 1877 :

"In my tour of inspection I have encountered so many great evils in the systems of various institutions that I feel impelled to recommend the propriety of this State following in the lead of other commonwealths, and enacting a law providing for the appointment of an Inspector of Public Institutions. The duties of this official should be to visit twice, or oftener in each year, every charitable, reformatory, or other institution in the State, supported wholly or in part by the public moneys: to thoroughly inspect and examine them, and report the result of his investigations to the Governor of the State. He should be empowered to redress all grievances which may come under his observation, and should, with that object in view, have free access to the records of each institution."

Those were my views at the time, and such views I expressed to Dr. Conrad. I do not believe he asked the question, but I also stated that I should do all that I could to have such a law passed, and that I would, myself, like to hold the position, inasmuch as I had begun the work, and see it thoroughly accomplished. He mentioned then something in regard to my position as president of the Spring Grove board of managers. I stated that I did not see that there was anything in that inconsistent with my still holding that position if it was desirable; that I could give all the time, when not employed in the duties of inspector of public charities, if I should receive such appointment under the proposed law, to the special duties of the hospital.

Q. You approached the Governor on that subject, did you not?

A. Yes, I spoke to him and told him that it would be an admirable thing.

Q. And he objected, did he?

A. He did not concur; I do not think he objected.

Q. Did I not say that that office would be inquisitorial or questionable, and that there would be great difficulty in passing such a law; that the State Board of Charities would be much more likely to be successful?

A. No, sir; I have not the slightest remembrance of that.

Q. Have you not said to me that you intended to have a law passed getting rid of certain members of the board?

A. I will state to the committee exactly what transpired. On several occasions Dr. Conrad spoke to me in reference to the members of the board, who, he said, were inimical to me, and on one occasion he spoke of a member of the board (Mr. McCoy, I don't know that he called his name either) but a member of the board, and I inferred who it was, who had stated to him that I took too much authority out there, and he thought I should confine myself more to my specific duties as president, or something to that effect. I then remarked that if such hostility as that exists in the board it is better that either I should quit or they should quit, and I was willing to submit the question to the legislature in regard to the matter. I never stated that I would have a law passed, because that would have been a piece of fatuity and folly of which I scarcely think I would have been guilty.

Q. Did you not subsequently tell me that at the next legislature there would be a reorganization of this present board?

A. No, sir, never; I stated to you, that if the difficulties which existed, or which I was told by Dr. Conrad, existed, I would lay the case before the legislature, and I thought I had friends in the legislature who would sustain me, and I believe I mentioned Mr. Gorman and Mr. Bannon.

Q. Were you and Dr. Brown not appointed as a committee on legislation by the board and instructed to draw up certain changes in the present organic law, which had been found, by experience, to work badly, and to submit them to the legislature, and to ask a repeal of those laws, and the enactment of those presented; and did not you and Dr. Brown come to Annapolis for that purpose?

A. I don't remember who the committee were; my impression is, that Gov. Bradford and Dr. Brown were on the committee. I did not come to Annapolis for that purpose.

Q. You were on the committee, were you not?

A. I was.

Q. Did you take any part in the changes proposed or requested?

A. I stated to Dr. Brown that he could have a bill prepared and I would look at it afterwards. The bill was afterward brought to my house by Governor Bradford and Mr. Compton, after it was prepared, and I stated to them that I concurred in the bill, and one reason that I concurred in it was, that the very first section provided for an entire reorganization of the board.

Q. Did you know at that time that there was a bill in the hands of Mr. Gorman for the reorganization of this board?

A. No, sir.

Q. Did you directly, or indirectly, have any hand or part in the construction of that bill that Mr. Gorman presented?

A. No, sir; only to advise with Mr. Gwynn and others with reference to certain portions of it, and give my views as to what I thought would be best for the interest of the hospital.

Q. At that very time, were you not on a committee appointed by your board to present to the legislature certain proposed changes in the organic law as it stood?

A. Yes, sir, I was on the committee.

Q. At the same time that you reviewed the bill now before the Senate?

A. I never reviewed it; I never saw it until after it was offered in the Senate and printed—not a word or line of it.

Q. I understood you to say just now that you had read certain sections of it with Mr. Gwynn?

A. No, sir; I said I had conferred with certain parties in regard to the matters contained in certain sections of the bill, and they may have put that in there from the advice which I gave, but I never saw the bill after it was prepared until it was in print.

Q. But you stated, at the same time, that you were on this committee to amend the present organic law.

A. Yes, sir.

Q. Did you, at any time, ask Mr. Brown, our present steward, to confer with Mr. Gorman concerning the change in this organic law, or concerning this present bill?

A. I don't remember that I did. I don't think that I saw Mr. Brown after the introduction of that bill until after it had been forwarded to me, printed, from Annapolis. I will tell you what I did do, I asked Mr. Brown when he was coming to Annapolis to speak to Mr. Gorman in reference to certain matters which I had suggested in regard to a change in the existing bill.

BY THE CHAIRMAN:

Q. What was defective in this bill of 1876 that you wanted amended?

A. There was one thing in regard to the treasurer. It was agreed by all that the superintendent should not hold the position of treasurer, and that the treasurer should be a member of the board. This law provided that no member of the board could be a paid officer, and no man would consent to perform the duties of treasurer without some compensation, and we all discussed that, and without reference to anybody being present, and without naming or thinking who would be treasurer, we all believed that the treasurer should be a member of the board, and that he should get a compensation of some three or four hundred dollars for his trouble; and we desired—at least I did—to have the law so changed that the treasurer might be a paid officer and a member of the board. In regard to the question of a quorum; we have had so much difficulty in get-ting a quorum of seven out of nine that I suggested an increased number of managers, and that those managers should come from different portions of the State, and that five should constitute a quorum instead of seven.

BY DR. CONRAD:

Q. Was that your suggestion in the changes proposed to

the present organic law, or was that the suggestion in connection with the present bill before the Senate?

A. I knew nothing about the present bill until I saw it in print. I made that suggestion, but whether it was put in the bill from my suggestion or not I cannot say.

BY THE CHAIRMAN:

Q. What became of that bill at Governor Bradford's house?

A. Dr. Brown brought it down here and presented it to somebody, I don't know whom. He told me that he was coming for that purpose. That is very little different from this bill, so far as I can see. It leaves it optional with the Board of Managers to establish by-laws in reference to the compensation of the treasurer. The important feature of this bill—and it is a matter upon which I conferred with Mr. Gwynn, and he wrote me a letter during my late sickness in regard to the matter, and spoke of the absolute necessity of taking action—is, the first section of the present bill. I believe that Mr. Gwynn drew up the entire bill which has been presented. I think I have heard that he did so, and that bill I never saw until it was in print and was sent to me in bill form. We have been annoyed by a suit for damages, of which mention is made in the report, and we speak of necessity for action by the legislature in regard to that matter. Mr. Gwynn thought the legislature should take such action as would stop these constant suits. Mr. Metz, who claims that he has been damaged by the driving off of his boarders, sued for one year when the old board had it, and then signified his intention of suing each year thereafter. His first suit was for fifty thousand dollars, and the jury gave him three hundred dollars damages. He then brought another suit, and I acknowledged service and communicated with Mr. Gwynn, who wrote me a note and requested me to call upon Mr. George Arthur Brown and get him to prepare a section of the bill. I did call upon him, and he forwarded me a section which he prepared, and which, I believe, though I could not say positively, is the section of the new bill.

By Dr. PERKINS:

Q. I understood you to say that the trouble of the board now was, to get a quorum of seven out of nine. What proportion of that nine reside in Baltimore city now?

THE WITNESS.

You mean appointed from the city?

Dr. PERKINS:

Yes.

A. There are six—Mr. Gunther, Dr. Thom, Mr. White, Mr. McCoy, Dr. Brown, and myself.

Q. If I understood you, the difficulty is in regard to securing a quorum of seven?

A. Yes, sir.

Q. Now you propose to increase the number. How many do you propose to increase it?

A. I did not specify the number, but I see it has been increased one by the bill.

Q. The idea is that you want them distributed over the State?

A. I think it would be better to distribute them over the State, so that the institution should have friends in every section of the State.

Q. How could you more readily get the quorum if the board was distributed over the whole State?

A. I proposed to have the quorum reduced from seven to five; that had no reference to the distribution at all.

Q. Then you would have a less number residing in Baltimore, but would not the difficulty of getting the quorum be still greater?

A. Permit me to say that I did not fix the number who should reside in Baltimore.

Q. I am asking your judgment, and am not inquiring about the prepared bill; what I want to get at is, how could you more readily obtain a quorum, if, as you suggest, the board was distributed all over the State in order to secure the interest of different parts of the State; whereas, you have now this difficulty when the majority reside in Baltimore.

10

A. I did not contemplate that so many from the city would be dropped; I contemplated that the board should be increased.

Q. Then a small number of the board would constitute a quorum?

A. Yes; because things often transpire which make it almost absolutely necessary to have a meeting of the board.

Q. Is it not unwise to let a small number of the Board of Directors, for an institution of this kind, control its affairs?

A. I think not, if you select men of good judgment.

Q. Of course; but why not confine it to them? Why have a great number, simply as complimentary, and then have the institution controlled by a small number?

A. I acknowledge that my idea was to popularize the institution, and get persons interested all over the State without reference to the business particularly.

By Mr. COMPTON:

Q. Did not the bill provide for the repeal of the entire act?

A. Yes, sir; it provided for the repeal of the entire chapter, and the enactment of the new law.

Q. Do you not remember that it provided further, that six should constitute a quorum instead of seven?

A. Yes, sir.

Q. Do you not remember that the board was a unit upon that matter of reducing the quorum?

A. Yes, sir.

By Dr. CONRAD:

Q. Did it provide for striking out the present portion of the law that forbids any member of the board from receiving any compensation?

A. It repealed the entire chapter.

Q. Then if it repealed the entire chapter, is this bill, as presented by this committee of which you and Dr. Brown were members, the same bill?

A. No, it is not. Dr. Brown's bill, I am sure, had nothing in reference to the suits of Metz, and nothing declaring that the institution had been, since its foundation, a State institution, which was intended to protect the institution against these suits.

Q. Then you have taken no part in endeavoring to advance the bill, as provided by the committee, of which you were a member?

A. I don't understand your question?

Q. You and Dr. Brown are members of this committee that provided this bill; you had been to the legislature in the interest of that bill provided by yourself and Dr. Brown?

A. I advised that the bill should be presented, and I still think that it would have been the best thing. I think that the bill that Dr. Brown sent here would have been the best bill in many respects, but it would have had to be amended by adding other sections to cover the ground I have just stated.

Q. You have taken no active part in advancing the passage of this bill?

A. No, sir, not any. This is the first time I have been to Annapolis since early in January.

By Dr. PERKINS:

Q. You wished that the treasurer should be a member of the board, and should receive compensation?

A. Yes, sir; I think the treasurer should be a member of the board.

Second Charge Read.

THE WITNESS:

Mr. Chairman, I cannot conceive how I ever converted the patronage of the hospital to my own political advantage. In regard to this transfer of groceries from Stump & Co., I will state that either the steward or Dr. Conrad told me that some fault was found with the purchases. Mr. Gunther was not in the city. I was a member of the purchasing committee with Mr. Gunther, and we concurred in giving an order for the purchase of groceries from Stump's. I was informed—I could not say whether by Dr. Conrad, or Brown, or the steward—that the groceries were not satisfactory. I then said, unhesitatingly, "Change your grocery man; we have no contract with Stump, and are under no

obligations to purchase groceries from him; if the groceries are not satisfactory, change." I spoke to Dr. Conrad
also in reference to the man, whom I believed to be a thoroughly honest man, as it was certainly my right to speak to
him when in the presence of Mr. Gunther or any one else.
I suggested that he should try Mr. Shawgo; that I had
purchased my groceries from him—a very small amount,
though—and I found him so entirely satisfactory and honest
that I believed it would be to the advantage of the hospital
to try him. I will state here, under oath, that at the time
I believed that Mr. Shawgo belonged to the Republican
party, and I never knew any difference until the other day
when he was down here, and I asked him whether he was
a Republican, and he said: "Doctor, I never cast but one
vote in my life, and that vote I cast for you." Dr. Conrad,
as Mr. Shawgo stated, went there and found the groceries
satisfactory. As to whether he ordered Mr. Brown to go
there and buy them, I do not know. Mr. Brown stated
that he did. There is one thing very certain, that I never
gave any order in reference to the matter. I did request
him to go there, and see what arrangement he could effect,
and whether it would be a judicious arrangement, and after
that they began to deal there. I admit that I am personally fond of this young man, Shawgo, and believe him to
be thoroughly honest; and, as he is beginning life, I was
anxious to aid him in any way that I could.

By Dr. CONRAD:

Q. Did you not say to me on several occasions to go to
Mr. Shawgo and examine his groceries with a view to changing the purchase of groceries from Stump & Co.?

A. I asked you to do so when those groceries were not
satisfactory. I do not remember of several occasions. I
believe I spoke to you twice; that is all I remember.

Q. Mr. Brown, the steward, spoke to me about some
grains of pepper being defective, but further than that I
never heard of the groceries being objectionable. I did go
to Mr. Shawgo, as the Doctor said. I was pleased with his

groceries and was pleased with Mr. Shawgo. Did you not direct me to make the change?

A. I never directed you. I requested you to go there if you found it judicious to make the change.

Q. I believe you acknowledged that all your orders were given in the shape of requests?

A. Yes, sir.

Q. Did you not then subsequently direct Mr. Brown to go there?

A. No, sir.

Third Charge Read.

THE WITNESS:

Mr. Chairman, I requested Dr. Conrad to go to Mr. Griffith's, and if he found that he could make his purchases there satisfactorily, I would like for him to do so, for the reason that young Mr. Griffith, the nephew of the gentleman who testified here the other day, and whose evidence I will state was accurate and correct throughout, asked me one day if we did not purchase a good many carpets at the hospital. I told him that we did, but I had very little to do with those matters. He said to me, " I wish you would give me some of the patronage of the institution." I said, " I have not the slightest objection to doing so, and I will speak to Dr. Conrad about it." I did so, and asked him to go there, and the Doctor said here the other day that he got carpets there cheaper by ten per cent. than at any other place. In regard to the latter part of the charge in reference to my countermanding the order, I said to Dr. Conrad, sometime in August or September, when the press and other parties were thundering into me so vehemently about my report, that I went to Mr. Griffith and told him, " You have visited the almshouses of the State and you must know that my statements are substantially correct, and I have come here to ask you to give me a letter, if you are willing to do so, substantiating my report." " Well," he said, " Doctor, you have written it in such a flowery way that I could not exactly endorse it." He said, " I can endorse a great deal that you do say, but some of the almshouses I found in a different condition, and, therefore, I could not give you a letter," and he mentioned especially Washington county.

Dr. Conrad asked me about purchasing carpets, and I said: "Doctor, you can get them where you please; I have no longer any preference for Mr. Griffith, because he had it in his power to relieve me in the estimation of the people of the State, and he would not do it." The facts are, that the carpets were purchased from Mr. Griffith. The purchases were made in the latter part of August, or early in September, and continued until the 5th of October, when the purchasing committee came back, and then Dr. Thom and Mr. Gunther, of the purchasing committee, made the purchases elsewhere. They notified me of the fact that they were going to make the change in the purchases, and I said to them that I had no desire in the matter, but that I would cheerfully concur in whatever they did in regard to them. They purchased the carpets, afterwards, in another place

By Dr. CONRAD:

Q. Did you not tell me to go to Mr. Griffith and purchase carpets; that you had bought carpets of him, and one special fact you stated was that he never sends a bill; that is, the credits are of long duration.

A. Yes, sir; that is so.

Q. You did state that?

A. Yes, sir; I believe I did. I had to go to him myself to get a bill; he never sent one to me.

Q. And I made the transfer in accordance with your directions?

A. Yes, sir; if you consider the request to go there and look at the carpets a direction.

Q. You acknowledge that your orders were given to me in the shape of requests usually.

A. I wish you would use the word "request" then; I prefer the word.

Q. Did you not subsequently approach me at the hospital upon the necessity of other purchases being made, and desire me to go to Turnbull's and get them; that you said : "I went to Griffith to get a letter of endorsement of my almshouse report and he would not give me one," and you made use of some epithet to him. Did you not then direct me to go back to Turnbull's, stating that Mr. Griffith had refused to give you this paper?

A. No, sir. I said you could go to Turnbull's or anywhere you pleased.

Q. But to leave Griffith's on that account?

A. No, sir; I said I no longer felt any interest in Griffith, and I had no desire for you to purchase carpets from him. Indeed, if I had expressed my personal feelings in the matter, I would have said I preferred you should not purchase them from him. Those were my feelings, and I don't disguise them.

By Mr. COMPTON:

Q. Do you know or not if carpets were bought from Griffith after this conversation?

A. Yes, sir.

Q. How long after?

A. The last purchase was the fifth of last October. They were bought there, but I do not know who bought them.

Q. You do know the fact that carpets were bought there after this conversation?

A. Yes, sir; Mr. Griffith himself stated that.

By Dr. CONRAD:

Q. You state that purchases were made of Griffith after that statement to me?

A. I take it from the books of the hospital.

Q. The date that you made that statement to me—you cannot make the statement under oath?

A. No, sir.

Dr. CONRAD:

Then withdraw that statement.

THE WITNESS:

I shall not withdraw any statement.

Q. How can you state that the purchases were continued after you made that statement to me?

A. Because I state that it was previous to the fifth of October that I had the conversation with you. It was immediately after my going to Mr. Griffith to secure this letter, or very soon thereafter, certainly within two weeks, and that was between the latter part of August and the first part of September.

Fourth Charge Read.

THE WITNESS:

Mr. Chairman, I did request Dr. Conrad recently to go to Mr. Dillehunt and purchase tobacco, and I will state here that I had introduced an ordinance in the City Council of Baltimore for the purpose of having certain insane patients transferred to Spring Grove from Bayview Asylum, where they had not the facilities of treating them properly, as the Board of Managers, or trustees, themselves acknowledged, because they were crowded there; but my chief object, I will admit, in introducing the ordinance for the transfer was to aid the Maryland Hospital. I wanted to build up the institution and fill it, if possible, with patients. In addition to the humanity, I admit that I felt very much interested in having the wards of the hospital filled, and I introduced this ordinance into the council, and I saw nearly every member of the council in person in regard to the matter. I spoke to Mr. Dillehunt about it, and he promised me that he would give me his aid in passing the ordinance in the Second Branch of the Council, of which he was a member. I was a member of the First Branch at the time. He did aid me and voted for it, and subsequently he came to me—I had never known what Mr. Dillehunt's business was before—he came to me and said that he apprehended that he might lose his patronage at Bayview, because the trustees were very much incensed at the passage of the ordinance. I asked him what his business was, and he told me that he was a tobacconist and that he had been supplying the Bayview institution with tobacco. I then said to him, "As far as it is in my power I will aid you in another way. We purchase a great deal of tobacco at the Maryland Hospital, and I am in favor always of aiding my friends.

You have been a friend of the institution, and I will speak to Dr. Conrad and ask him to communicate with you in regard to this matter, and if he finds that your charges are no greater than those of others, I will ask him to purchase tobacco of you." I did so, and Dr. Conrad subsequently came to me and told me, I think, that Mr. Dillehunt's charges were higher, and I said to him, immediately, "Don't hesitate to change, change immediately." It was no condition for his voting for the ordinance that we should purchase tobacco of him, because he had already voted for it. This was sometime after the ordinance had passed, and I said I only promised to deal with Mr. Dillehunt if his charges were no greater than at other places.

Fifth Charge Read.

THE WITNESS:

Mr. Chairman, the committee have heard the statement of Dr. Dulaney in regard to this matter. I will state here that he never gave me any money to aid in my election, except as he stated, for campaign purposes. He sent me one hundred dollars, without my solicitation. He went to a gentleman in the ward and offered him the money, and he said to Mr. Dulaney, "You had better give that money to Dr. Chancellor, who is the treasurer of the ward organization, and all money contributed for ward purposes should go into his hands." Mr. Dulaney then brought me the one hundred dollars and told me it was for the purpose of aiding in the existing campaign.

By Dr. CONRAD:

Q. Did you not tell me to transfer the account from Kelly & Piet to Dulaney, stating at the same time, as a reason, that the latter had given you one hundred dollars to aid in your election?

A. No, sir; I never said anything about my own election; I said to aid in campaign purposes; but I did request you to transfer.

Q. Did you not make use of the expression, "Aid in my election?"

A. No, sir; I requested you to try Dulaney, and if you found that his goods were equal to others it would be personally gratifying to me if you would deal with him. I do not hesitate to say that, because I admit that a friend of mine or a friend of my party, I will always sustain in preference to other people, provided no injustice is done.

Sixth Charge Read.

THE WITNESS:

I told Mr. Gunther that Dr. Conrad informed me that he would require two more horses at the hospital. Mr. Gunther said, "I know nothing about horses—you do, I know you do, and I will sanction any purchase that you make." I stated to a horse-dealer that I desired to purchase a pair of horses. He sent three or four pair of horses to my house for me to see. I rejected all, and finally he sent a very fine pair of young iron-gray horses of the Normandy stock that I thought would suit the hospital admirably. They were perfectly sound in every respect, and have proved so. They have been there nearly a year, I think; but I was satisfied from my own knowledge of horseflesh that they were sound and good horses. I had rejected three or four previously, because I did not like them. He asked me six hundred dollars for this pair. I told him I would not pay over four hundred dollars; that I thought that was enough for them, and I thought they were cheap enough at that. He hooted at the idea of four hundred dollars for them and went off. A few days afterward he came to me and said that he had concluded to take five hundred dollars, but I said, "No, sir, I would not give you four hundred dollars and one cent for them. I will give you four hundred dollars and no more." Then, the third time, the owner of the horses came. I did not know until that moment but what the horse-dealer owned the horses. The owner brought them himself this time, and he proved to be a man who lived in my ward, and he said, "Doctor, I have concluded to take four hundred dollars for those horses." I remember distinctly asking him if the horses belonged to him, and he said, " Yes." I said then, " I must try the horses for a day or two: I want to drive them myself before I buy." He said, " Very well." It was the day of a visit of a committee, or the entire council, I do not know which, to Spring Grove—a committee I think—for some purpose in regard, probably, to this matter of transferring patients from Bay-view. I hitched the horses to my own carriage and got Mr. Ober, who is a gentleman of good judgment, to drive out with me to the hospital. We drove out and Mr. Ober said he was very much pleased with the horses, and said he thought they would be exceedingly cheap at four hundred dollars. After we got out there we called the attention of several members of the board to the horses, and they exam-ined them and advised me to purchase. Mr. Compton also did, I think. I went back the next morning and closed the bargain with the owner of the horses, and sent them out to the hospital, and the horses have proved to be sound in every respect, I believe.

Seventh Charge Read.

THE WITNESS:

This question has been already discussed here, I believe. I have stated that Dr. Conrad stated to me the urgent ne-cessity of these repairs, and I sent a plumber out there to do the work. The pipes were leaking, and the ceilings injured. I did not deem it necessary to consult the executive committee about a matter that was so obviously necessary. Though, when my attention was called to the fact that I had not consulted them, I went immediately and found two members of the committee, Mr. McCoy, I think, and Mr. White, and stated that I had ordered this plumbing to be done, and they sanctioned it. Did I not speak to you about it, Mr. White?

MR. WHITE:

Oh, yes; and I thought you were justified, under the cir-cumstances, in doing it.

DR. CONRAD [to the witness]:

Who called your attention to it?

A. I think, probably, you did.

Q. Did I not state that the plumbers had said that the bill would amount to about twelve hundred dollars ?

A. I don't remember that.

Q. And when it was found that it belonged to the executive committee, did I not state that, in order to avoid difficulty, you had better consult with Mr. McCoy?

A. I don't remember about the twelve hundred dollars, but I do remember that you called my attention to the fact that I should have consulted the committee, and I went, immediately after that, and consulted the executive committee. But the bill of the men for this plumbing was six hundred dollars, which we have since paid.

Q. Was there not a good deal of objection to the charges of that bill?

A. There were objections as to certain items. Gov. Bradford, as a member of the committee, objected to several •items of the bill, for instance. item of solder, and the price per day for plumbing help. An investigation was made subsequent to his objection, and Gov. Bradford and Mr. Compton both came to the conclusion, after consulting other plumbers, that the man had not charged too much for first-class work. They then, as the finance committee, approved his bill for six hundred dollars.

By Mr. ACTON.

Q. How much per day was charged?

A. I think it was four dollars for plumbers, and two dollars for help; I am not sure about that, but that is my impression. The bill went into the hands of the finance committee and I never looked at it.

By Dr. THOM:

Q. Was not that bill deemed, at first sight, inordinate, but was it not found. upon investigation. that those charges were made larger by reason of their having to come from the city to the hospital, thereby involving more expense?

A. No, sir; the only question in regard to that was that these parties who did the work boarded at Catonsville, and a charge was made for board, to which Gov. Bradford objected. I myself, as one of the committee, thought it incorrect.

However, I went to see other mechanics, and asked them what the usage was in such cases, and each one of them told me that where board had to be paid the employers invariably paid the board. I stated this to the committee, and they then unhesitatingly audited the bill.

BY THE CHAIRMAN:

Q. Who was this plumber?

A. Patrick Cary.

Eighth Charge Read.

THE WITNESS:

I have just made a full statement in regard to that.

Ninth Charge Read.

THE WITNESS:

I have not visited the hospital from the latter part of November until the ninth day of March. If the committee desire me to state the reasons for not going, I will do so.

THE CHAIRMAN:

It is not desired, unless it is by Dr. Conrad.

Tenth Charge Read.

THE WITNESS:

I sent the oysters out there by a man. I do not remember of having ordered them to be sent out. A request was made to me to send out a waiter and a gallon of oysters. He is a public waiter, and also keeps an oyster cellar, and was a good man. Indeed, he was a servant in my house a long time, and was certainly a most trustworthy man. Some objection was made to him here, I believe, by the steward, but he was in my house for a long time as my own waiter, and he kept my keys, and had access to liquors and everything else, and I never knew the man to take a drink of liquor in my life. I directed him to go out to the hospital upon this occasion and take with him the oysters, and he has been out there several times, since by my orders, I believe.

Eleventh Charge Read.

No one desired to ask any questions.

Twelfth Charge Read.

THE WITNESS:

I want to go a little into details there. On one occasion, on a visit to the hospital to see Dr. Conrad, as a friend—this was before I qualified as a member of the board, and certainly long before the organization of the board (it was sometime in the latter part of March or first April, and the board was organized on the 7th of July following—the Doctor invited me to go with him to the green-house, and he made some statement about the number of plants which was sold there. I took very little note of it, because I was not particularly interested in the hospital at that time. He offered to send me some rose cuttings and some geraniums, &c. I remember distinctly that I told him I did not like to receive anything from a public institution, but that I was willing to pay for such things, as I would have to buy them elsewhere. He said he would not accept pay, and mentioned the fact that members of the board were in the habit of getting such things as they wanted. He sent to my country place a box containing some roses and geraniums, and some other little things. I think I could have bought the whole number that was sent for two dollars or two dollars and fifty cents anywhere. One day, subsequent to that, when I was out at the hospital, I saw the gardener and told him that the plants had been received, and complimented him upon his flowers and plants; and I said that Dr. Conrad would not receive pay for them, and I wanted to make him some compensation, and so I gave him five dollars. I did not give it to him for the hospital, I gave it to him for himself. That is all in reference to this charge, except that last summer I was out at the hospital, and the gardener was trimming blackberry bushes, and I asked him to save me a few cuttings, and said I would like to plant them at my place. He did so, and sent me also one hundred tomato plants, I think, in the same box. Of course I never thought of offering to pay for them; they were but a small matter. That is the extent of my peculations upon the institution.

By Dr. CONRAD:

Q. Did not that last box contain a large assortment of rose-cuttings?

A. I did not see the box when it was opened. If it contained them they were put in of your own accord.

Q. Do you not remember of sending me a list of such articles?

A. I believe I sent you a list and told you that I would be glad to have those things. I remember that now, though I do not know what was on the list.

Q. You say you were not a member of the board at the first shipment?

A. No, sir.

Dr. CONRAD:

I think your commission will show. At any rate the law shows that it was passed on the 7th of April. There was some delay in obtaining the commissions by the different members of the board, but they were obtained before the 1st of June, I am sure, and I think in the month of May, and Mr. Hall died, I think, about July 1st.

THE WITNESS:

He died in June.

Dr. CONRAD:

I think it was July.

THE WITNESS:

I can tell when he was buried [referring to memorandum]. C. W. Hall, gardener, was buried 25th June, 1876.

Q. What is the date of your commission?

A. I do not know what the date was, but I did not consider myself a member of the board until it was organized. I had no authority to act as a member until it was organized.

Q. Did you not visit the hospital as a member of the board before that time?

A. I was frequently out there, but I assumed no authority until after the organization of the board.

By Dr. PERKINS:

Q. Those cuttings were made where they were trimming up the blackberry bushes?

A. I suppose so. They were sent down to my place. but I did not see them at the time. The roses were little slips in pots and settings of the year previous. There were one or two of that size [measuring on his hand]. I saw them after they were planted. and the others were small things.

By Mr. HOUSTON:

Q. In reference to those last cuttings, would they have been thrown away if they had not been given to you?

A. I cannot say, because I did not see them. I only requested him to send me some cuttings.

Q. They would have been of no value to the institution if you had not taken them?

A. I do not suppose they would have been of any value to the institution.

The committee adjourned to 4 o'clock P. M., Monday, March 25, 1878.

The testimony of John W. McCoy, in the matter of charges brought by Dr. Conrad against Dr. Chancellor, before the Maryland Legislative Committee on Public Buildings.

FIRST. So far as I know, friendly relations existed between Dr. Chancellor and Dr. Conrad up to November last. Since that time this amity has been utterly broken up. A rupture sprang out of the fact that Dr. Conrad's annual report did not agree, on some important point, with the annual report of the board, made by Dr. Chancellor. This offended Dr. Chancellor and dissatisfied the board. Dr. Conrad afterward modified his report, so as to do away with the leading points of discord between it and Dr. Chancellor's report. In discussing the matter in committee, Dr. Conrad was invited in, and, among other remarks, said: "Dr. Chancellor, you must pardon me for saying that it was highly improper for the board to adopt your report without reading mine. In all hospitals the board's report must be necessarily based on the report of the superintendent, on account of his constant and intimate knowledge of the patients and the daily administration." This remark gave offence to Dr.

Chancellor and one other member of the committee. As time passed on the breach widened, until there was open bitterness between Dr. Chancellor and Dr. Conrad. Three or four members of the board used continued endeavor for peace and the avoidance of scandal. In the meantime Dr. Chancellor, for several months, absented himself from the hospital.

Dr. Conrad finally addressed the board a letter, respectfully asking definite knowledge as to whom and in what way he was charged with offending, disclaiming any intention of offence, and volunteering to make reparation when he should be shown to have given just ground of offence. This letter was referred to a special committee, consisting of Mr. Compton, Governor Bradford and myself. Dr. Conrad met us upon notification, and the ground of his offence was fully stated to him, and it was arranged by unanimous agreement of the committee that Dr. Conrad should address them a letter conveying his views and feelings. Dr. Conrad then sent to the committee a letter of such character that it was by them unanimously approved, as all that the occasion called for. Mr. Compton pronounced it as brave and manly a letter as he had ever read, and to me he said, that it should be entirely satisfactory to Dr. Chancellor. Govorner Bradford arose at the board, warmly commended it, its earnest appeal for peace, and Dr. Conrad's cordial manner at the interview. Mr. Farnandis turned to Dr. Chancellor and said, "Doctor, there is everything in that letter that an honorable man can say. If a letter can do anything, that letter ought to do it." Other members of the board were equally emphatic in their approval, and it was finally approved by the board without a dissenting vote, even Dr. Chancellor saying that he would " Let the matter rest until after the adjournment of the legislature." But the matter was not suffered to rest. Dr. Thom told me at the hospital, shortly afterward, that the matter was not settled; that Dr. Chancellor would never again come to the hospital while Dr. Conrad was there; that he (Dr. Thom) had told Dr. Chancellor that it was wrong to stay away; that as president, his visits there were matters of plain duty; but that he was sure Dr. Chancellor would not visit the hospital while Dr. Conrad was there; that one or the other would have to leave it.

This state of things continued until Dr. Thom and Mr. Compton brought the matter again before the board upon the ground that trouble must ensue from discordant government, and that either Dr. Chancellor or Dr. Conrad would have to quit the administration. At this meeting (seven members present) Mr. Compton, Dr. Thom and Governor Bradford said if Dr. Chancellor left the board they would leave with him. There was no definite action and no vote at this meeting, but it was plain that Dr Conrad's resignation would be acceptable to the gentlemen above named. I could not concur in this view, as my constant observation, as chairman of the executive committee, compelled me to regard Dr. Conrad's connection with the hospital as of vastly more importance to it and to its inmates than that of any member of the board. There was no record of the uttered sentiment of this meeting, and no one was authorized to advise Dr. Conrad of it. Dr. Brown, however, at once went to the hospital, and suggested to Dr. Conrad that his resignation might save him from a more painful procedure. Dr. Brown stated afterward at the board, in my presence, that Dr. Conrad declined to resign without an official request, and that Dr. Conrad then took from his pocket a paper containing charges against his assistant, Dr. Broome. The board was convened to consider this paper, an earnest debate ensued, an early day was fixed for trial, and here (in point of time) ends my personal knowledge, for, from imperative engagements already made, it was impossible for me to be at the trial.

Regarding Dr. Conrad's specific charges, I testify as follows:

CHARGE No. 1. Dr. Chancellor, before the board originally organized, asked me aside at Barnum's and said that Dr. Conrad was a good hospital physician, but that he had no business capacity: that he (Dr. Chancellor) had spent

almost his whole adult life in hospitals, and knew well how
to economize; that Spring Grove could be conducted at a
vastly decreased expense, but that he (Dr. Chancellor) would
not live there for ten thousand dollars a year. Now there
was nothing whatever in the law of 1876 requiring the
superintendent to live at Spring Grove. This was afterward fixed by the by-laws. The strong impression made
upon me by this conversation was, that Dr. Chancellor
would like the superintendency himself if the board would
not exact residence at the hospital. This I mentioned to
two or three members of the board, as I had a perfect right
to do, and Dr. Brown concurred in my inference and said so
emphatically. What he told Dr. Conrad of this matter, as
stated by Dr. Conrad, I have no knowledge of.

CHARGE No. 2. My testimony is, that at a meeting of the
board last autumn, bills were presented amounting to about
one thousand two hundred dollars, which Mr. Gunther,
chairman of the purchasing committee, then said he had
never given any order for. Mr. Gunther complained that
the goods thus bought, without his authority, were from
retailers who could not sell except at higher prices than
larger dealers, whom he had selected for supplies.

CHARGES 3, 4, 5 AND 6. Of these I know nothing.

CHARGE No. 7. When I was summoned to the hospital
concerning the need of plumbing, I went at once. After
carefully inspecting the building in company with Dr. Chancellor and Dr. Conrad (Dr. Chancellor having already a
plumber on the ground), I, on behalf of the executive committee, authorized special plumbing work, not to exceed
one hundred dollars. At a subsequent board-meeting, the
plumber's bill presented was for about six hundred dollars.

CHARGE No. 8. In my presence and that of Dr. Brown,
at my office, Dr. Chancellor denied ever having expressed
any wish or determination to get rid of any member of the
board. Dr. Brown told me, that on leaving my office with
Dr. Chancellor, the latter had said that if he ever had used any
such expression it was in temper, and not with any purpose.

CHARGE No. 9. This I know only from never meeting

Dr. Chancellor at the hospital since November last: from Dr. Conrad's statement that he had not been there; and from Dr. Thom's statement to me that he would not go there.

CHARGES 10, 11, 12 AND 13. Of these I have no knowledge.

REGARDING MR. BANNON's INQUIRY ABOUT THE COAL PURCHASE, my knowledge is. that the executive committee, by authority of the board. had made a contract with Messrs. Bartlett, Robbins & Co., to refit the hospital heating apparatus, so that they would guarantee it to consume a greatly diminished amount of coal; that when the coal was being hauled out, this firm protested to me more than once against the quality of the coal as making compliance with their contract impossible. On their final and emphatic protest, I at once took their representative to Mr. Gunther, chairman of the purchasing committee, who said—" You know, Mr. McCoy, that is the coal Dr. Chancellor bought. I will see him about it." The complainant said to Mr. Gunther and myself that the coal was so bad that it would rate in the market a dollar and a half a ton less than good engine coal. Mr. Francis White and I, visiting the hospital on inspection day. Dr. Thom joined us, looked at large masses of coal in the pits, and pronounced it very bad. After a large delivery of this sort the quality was improved, so as to stop Messrs. Bartlett, Robbins & Co.'s objections.

JOHN W. McCOY.

BALTIMORE, March 24th, 1878.

State of Maryland, Baltimore City, to wit:

On this 25th day of March, 1878, before me, the subscriber, one of the Justices of the Peace in and for the State and city aforesaid. personally appeared John W. McCoy, and made oath on the Holy Evangely of Almighty God. that the annexed statements, made by him, of nine pages, concerning the affairs of the Maryland Hospital for the Insane, are true to the best of his knowledge and belief.

Sworn before   WM. S. GORTON,
        Justice of the Peace for the Third Ward of Baltimore city.